Wet Heat Collection 1-3

A BLUE COLLAR BEST FRIENDS SISTER BILLIONAIRE ROMANCE

KEKE RENÉE

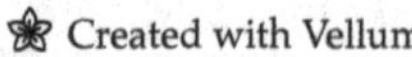

Latest Releases By Keke Renée:

- Wet Heat (Wet Heat Series Book 1)
- Every Time We Touch Novelette (Wet Heat Book 2 Series)
- His Peace, Her Pleasure
- Baby, It's Cold Outside
- Love Don't Live Here Anymore, Vanessa Andrew Book 1
- Love Don't Live Here Anymore, Isabella Andrew Book2
- One Night Only-A Novelette (Love By Design Book 1)
- Cassian and Savannah (Love By Design Book 2)
- Deidra's Love (Love By Design Book 3)
- Protecting Bria (Special Force Operation Alphas)
- Sensual
- Seek To Please Book 1
- Seek To Touch Book 2
- Seek To Bare Book 3
- Seek To Love Book 4
- Protecting Chanel (Special Forces Operation Alphas)
- Seek To Trust Book 5
- Seek To Earn Book 6

Chelsey Hayden lives by strict codes under her family's name. When you're a Hayden, you follow the rules and never stray from the course they have had laid out for you since birth; especially when it comes to her brother's friends being off limits, no matter how handsome and sexy they are. That is until the rules of the game change, and she crosses paths with the one she wants to break all the rules for, but she's scared – scared she'll reveal her deepest, darkest desires and then there will be no turning back.

Xavier Hardy is a man from a humble beginning, working a nine to five while paying off debt and taking care of his family. Falling for his best friend's sister wasn't in the cards. He knows what he wants and isn't afraid to chase after it, and right now, he wants Chelsey, the curvaceous beauty he can't get out of his head. Now if only he could convince her to explore her desires and give in to temptation.

If lust takes over, this once off-limits relationship could spiral out of control. Are they ready to challenge the rules and simply enjoy the ride?

Introduction

I'm beyond excited for you to read this book, and beyond thankful that you've chosen my books as some to include on your shelf. Let me know what you think and follow me on Goodreads, Bookbub, and my Facebook for all the latest.

Are you signed up for my newsletter?

Join today and find out all the latest in new releases, contests, giveaways, sneak peeks and so much more.

https://dl.bookfunnel.com/wmpxcjxsps

Thank you so much for reading and enjoying this crazy ride with Xavier & Chelsey.

I WANT TO THANK first all of my readers for loving these characters so much and supported my entire journey. Family for supporting and helping along this author world.

Disclamier

THIS WORK OF FICTION contains strong language and explicit sexual content and is only intended for mature readers. This story may contain unconventional situations, language, and sexual encounters that may offend some readers. This book is for mature readers (18+).

PART

One

Preface

"I like that," she whispered as I caressed her nipples. I smiled and looked her in the eyes and whispered, "You are magnificent, how are you so perfect?" I kissed her softly as she threw her arms around my neck pulling me down to her, and increasing the passion of our kiss.

"Is this okay?" I asked as I began to lightly run my fingertips down her chest drifting under the sheet, caressing over her voluptuous breasts and hard nipples, all the way down her belly, and thighs.

I desperately wanted to sink my cock into her sweet, tight, juicy pussy, but knew I wouldn't last long if I did. My genuine desire to pleasure her first compelled me to take it slow, drawing it out and just kissing and caressing her for a while. Eventually, reaching her mound, I felt her warm heat seeping through. I ghosted my touch around her outer lips teasing and tantalizing as I went, gauging her reaction before slipping a finger into her slit,

"Oh, yes, Xavier please," She moaned, sinking her nails in my ass cheeks.

CHAPTER

One

CHELSEY

"I WANNA FUCK YOU," I whispered, hoping my parents wouldn't hear as they sat across from us at the dining room table in our family home. No, too creepy. 'Let's fuck!' Way too straight-forward, even for my taste. 'I've had my eyes on you for a while?' Hell no, I'm not a fucking stalker. I thought to myself.

I contemplated what to say as we ate breakfast and caught up with each other at brunch. Struggling to make up my mind on what was the best approach, I decided to drop by Xavier's gym before work and take it from there. Sitting across from him as he talked and ate with my family gave me goosebumps every time. If he could look at me as a person, and not just as Jordan's little sister, I know we could have something special. Xavier always worked late on Thursdays, if I surprise him with dinner and confess my long overdue feelings of love. Would he see me as more than my family's name?

"Chelsey, what time are you heading to the bank today? Jordan asked.

"Probably about ten, I wanted to get an early workout in first," I answered and looked over at Xavier not making eye contact with me. I started to feel foolish for even thinking he'd want me.

"Okay cool, maybe you can catch a ride with me since I'm going to the gym first and then the office myself."

I rolled my eyes at my brother offering to crash my little surprise I had in store for Xavier. He's one of the reasons why I'm twenty-eight and unmarried; every time I get close to someone either my parents or my brother gets involved and breaks us up. I did eventually lose my virginity to my high school boyfriend. It became this covert operation with purchasing the perfect outfit, staying late after school to give my parents time to get home. I lied and said I was staying with a girlfriend when actually I snuck around and spent the night with the most popular guy in high school, Ronnie Jasper.

He was sweet, making sure to please me first before just jumping my bones. He wasn't a virgin, and never made me feel like I needed to be something I'm not. We lasted another six months and then my brother caught us kissing at school one day and snitched to my dad, scaring him away. I remember hearing that he went off to Arizona State College, and then playing professional ball with Arizona Cardinals.

"No thank you. I'll drive myself," I replied and took a sip of my orange juice. After a while, he would learn when I put my foot down to let me grow up and see me as a strong, independent, and confident woman.

"Baby, maybe you should let Jordan drive you. It's on his way, and you could save on gas money," Dad stated.

Gerald Hayden is the type of man that speaks, and everyone listens including his children. Don't get me wrong growing up in my family has its blessings, we've established ourselves in the town as a family that not only works hard with generational wealth, but we give back to the community. My grandparents on my dad's side opened the first bank in Memphis, TN around 1949 and then passed it down to my dad. On my mom's side, Lynidas Champion is the epitome of beauty, class, and education.

Before getting married, she was the Dean of Admissions at Yale and met my father on a business trip. They fell in love and had my brother Jordan, who thinks he's God's gift to women. I remember growing up with girls constantly bickering and calling our phone wanting to know where Jordan was and who he was with.

Now he's engaged to my best friend, Emma Turner. Surprisingly we have the same shape, and if you know Jordan, he's never been the type to date girls with curves. We work at the same job, but Emma's a little feistier than me. She can put Jordan in his place, and I guess that made him see her in a different light because she didn't fall all over him. Yes, I hooked them up. It was by accident one day when I couldn't pick up Jordan from the airport because of work, and she offered to go in my place, and they got to talking and hit it off. Now two years later, they were planning to get married.

"Excuse me; I have to go get ready. Thanks for breakfast Lily," I said, to the family maid, ignoring my father and kissed her on the cheek, before heading toward my bedroom. This was the day I would finally tell Xavier how I felt, and no one would stand in the way. We've talked in the past, and he's told me about past girlfriends, and I've spoken about my past relationships and how my parents try to control my love life. I entered my old bedroom since I stayed here over the weekend after my parents threw a charity event. I decided to sleep here and leave for work the next day.

Now that I've gotten the basics of my plan all thought out, I needed to find a way to make Xavier feel something for me, or at the very least get him horny.

"What better way to make him interested than through

my clothes?" I figured. "I'll pick something that shows off what I've got, but still keeps him guessing. It'll have to be gym slash 'I want you to lick me from my head to my toes'-appropriate as well."

I eventually decided to go with my favorite pair of blue tights, with mesh cutouts on the sides, and a form-fitting blue halter crossbody top with just a little bit of cleavage. I packed a black skirt suit to change into after working out. I was fully aware that my body does not conform to society's standards, but I also knew very well that I could still pull the "tight-clothes" look off. I wasn't stick-thin, but still a bit on the toned side.

I looked in the full-length mirror in my closet, seeing my dark skin glowing with the new Fenty foundation. I couldn't help but feel proud of my curves. My perky ass was sitting upright even though I haven't worked out in over two months and was a size sixteen; I could still catch a few eyes. Somehow my stomach stayed flat and legs toned. The shirt showed off every curve of my frame - not to mention my gorgeous 40C boobs that had not sagged a centimeter since I was a teenager.

With the outfit settled, I moved on to make up. I usually liked to go a bit overboard with my face, from the foundation, eyeliner, blush, concealer. Sometimes late at night I would watch YouTube makeup tutorials to keep up to date with the products... Unfortunately, since today was a regular work day after working out, it would have to stay professional. I wasn't prepared to risk hearing any snide comments from my nosy coworkers and blabbing to my brother and father at the bank where I worked.

So what to do? It had to be sexy, but still professional. Eventually, I decided on just putting a little extra effort into my usual daily routine. I applied the basics; primer, foundation, and concealer. I didn't bother with any lipstick this time, just lip gloss; it wouldn't feel right in the office to look as though I'm heading to a concert rather than work.

"Perfect," I said and smacked my lips. "Looking hot, Chelsey."

I can say one good thing about my parents besides being strict to the bone, they instilled self-love, and every day in the morning my mom or dad would have me look in the mirror and remind myself of how beautiful I am and to never let anyone else's standards of beauty define me. Those words went a long way, especially on a day like today. I knew Xavier wouldn't be able to resist me looking like this, and that it'd be worth it.

———

"How do I look, Emma?" I asked, checking my makeup before getting out of the car. I begged my best friend to come with me for an early workout, and she forced me to take her to lunch afterward on my break. That's the best part of working for a family owned business. I set my own schedule.

"You look like someone trying to get laid at nine-fifteen in the morning. Tell me again why I agreed to this?" she questioned, as she stepped out of the car heading inside. We showed our passes and headed to the locker room to put our things up.

"Emma, sometimes I question how we became friends. Ever since you got engaged to my brother, you've become a homebody. I can never get you out of the house anymore," I said, motioning for her to walk in front of me toward Xavier's class.

"Don't blame this on your brother, actually scratch that you can. I think I'm pregnant," Emma said, standing in the back of the class, placing her mat down.

"Are you serious? Congratulations, you don't seem too

excited. What's wrong?" I questioned, and released her from a hug, noticing her quiet demeanor.

Xavier walked inside, and my entire body froze; we made eye contact, and he smiled back at me. I think it was too late to change my panties after seeing his large muscles through the t-shirt, and the workout shorts showing his large girth. Damn, I mumbled to myself.

"If you stare any longer, you'll give yourself away. Did we come here to work out or stare at your boo?" Emma asked, nudging me to move over a little.

Waving her off, I stood on my mat waiting to get directions. He turned the music down and instructed everyone to pick up the weights.

"I didn't tell your brother about the baby," Emma said, mumbling under her breath.

"What's going on Emma? Jordan would love to have kids with you," I replied.

"We can talk about it later over lunch. For now, check out your man, he hasn't taken his eyes off you since he walked in."

Looking over at Xavier, jealousy crept up watching him teach another woman how to stand with the weights; his hands were on her elbow and back. A part of me wanted to be her and have his hands on me, and the other part of me wanted to slap him for even showing off what belongs to me. If I can see the large print in his shorts, then other women noticed it sitting firmly on his thigh.

CHAPTER

Two

XAVIER

I WATCHED her lift the weights one at a time, moaning in pain while bent over the barstool and showing off her round, plump ass. An ass that will belong to me soon and just the mere sight of it encased in those tights had me brick hard and wanting to cancel class. I knew Chelsey had a crush on me, shit I've been in love with her since the first time we met in high school.

I'm best friends with her brother, and even though my family's not upper-class wealthy, they never made me feel beneath them. Not yet anyway. Jordan used to go to private schools when he was younger, and he acted out and got into trouble, he begged his parents to let him go to public school and that's how we met.

Over the years our families became friends, and they've helped me out from time to time whenever my parents argued, and during those times I was left home alone with no food, Mom crying in her room, and Dad heading off to go gamble with the rent money. Jordan caught on quickly to the routine of my parents fighting, and he asked if it happened often. I couldn't hide what was going on, and I tried to avoid the subject. One day the fight was so explosive the cops were called. I'd find myself at Jordan's home with his family.

After turning eighteen, I picked up a job at the gym, I was there all the time anyway since working out helped to ease the pain of hearing my parents argue. Knowing the type of toxic relationship, I grew up around, dating and being in relationships was something I avoided at all costs. Sex is what I'm all about, and the women in my past can admire my special skills. Getting Chelsey on board may be a little harder than I thought since she's a virgin. You wonder how I know.

She thought Jordan was the one responsible for messing up her relationships and dating life. I was the one that mentioned the idea; every time she got close with someone, we'd either crash her date or scare the guy off. After a while, she didn't tell anyone she was dating until her parents had an event and they came together. Just the thought of someone touching her and kissing her perfect pouty lips, running their hands up and down her thick thighs made me jealous. "Fuck!" I shouted.

"Huh?" Chelsey asked with a confused expression on her face.

"Uh, sorry, I slammed the barbell down too hard," I replied, hesitating for a moment looking at the stares from the other women. If you knew me, you'd know that I was the top trainer at the gym, all the women wanted me, but I only had eyes for Chelsey.

I loved that she was bite size, and I could pick her up, and let her juices drizzle down my face when I'm caressing her with my tongue. I pictured her lips wrapped around my nine inches with her eyes staring up at me in love. Being thirty years old with no experience in relationships, meant I had to have all my ducks in a row if I wanted her to be mine. The sweat glistened off her warm chocolate skin and down her chest. Just imagining our bodies pressed together. I licked my lips ready to devour her in front of everyone, and then remembered a full class was waiting on the next instructions.

"Alright class that's it for the day. Remember tomorrow same time nine-thirty," I said, ushering everyone out before I jumped Chelsey's bones in front of the entire room.

"Uhm, Xavier can I ask you something?" Chelsey asked, fidgeting with her hands, nervously looking around to see if someone was listening to our conversation.

"Sure, anything for you Peanut," I said and smiled as Chelsey rolled her eyes at the nickname Jordan and I gave her when she was younger.

She crossed her arms over her chest, pushed up her large breasts, and stood with her butt poking out tapping her feet. I liked when she got upset, something inside of me loved seeing the fire in her eyes and knowing I could draw that reaction out of her turned me on even more.

"First don't call me, Peanut. Second of all, dinner tonight with me at eight o'clock. Don't be late and wear something sexy," Chelsey answered, biting her bottom lip and smirking. She patted my chest and walked out swishing her hips seductively from side to side, so I'd notice her fine ass.

Shaking my head at her exit routine, I finished cleaning up and picked up my ringing phone noticing it was one of my sex buddies. They know not to call me; I call them when I need a night of fun. "It better be important," I answered on the third ring.

"Xavier, baby I need you," Teresa moaned out over the phone.

"Teresa, are you playing with yourself?" I questioned.

Hearing rustling on the other end, I got annoyed with her constant pressure of trying to make us into a couple.

"Baby, she misses you. Why can't we make it official?" Teresa asked.

"Because you know what this is, and what you agreed on was us being fuck buddies and nothing else. I don't do relationships."

"Unless you're Chelsey Hayden I bet," Teresa mumbled.

"I suggest you keep her name out of your mouth if you want to continue this little arrangement. Do I make myself clear?"

"Fine. How about you come over and feed me that big dick of yours and put me to sleep," Teresa replied.

It had to be the last time I slept with Teresa if I want to get serious with Chelsey. I refuse to lose her before I confessed my feelings. Her parents have a loving relationship, maybe I could talk with her father about my intentions.

"X...Xavier ...mmmhmm," Teresa groaned.

"Yeah, give me twenty minutes," I replied.

"I'm ending things tonight," I thought to myself, as I texted Chelsey to find out where this dinner is happening.

Me: Peanut, am I meeting you for dinner or picking you up?

Chelsey: My place at 8 pm and don't be late (winky emoji)

"Damn."

CHAPTER

Three

CHELSEY

"HEY XAVIER, THANKS FOR COMING," I said.

I stood at the door wearing a long red dress that teased my every curve. It was sleeveless with the back cutout and zipped up around my neck. I went to the hairstylist and had her put my hair up in a tight bun, with a few curls hanging low. The dress had a split all the way up to my right thigh; this was my chance to make an impression with him to not see me as the little girl running behind him and my brother. To notice me as a woman that knows what she wants even if she may have to hide this from her family.

He had on a black suit with a black shirt with the three top buttons loose with no tie. His mouth hung open, and that was the reaction I was going for in more ways than one.

"Are you coming inside?" I asked, holding the door and stepping aside. He handed me pink roses and kissed me on the forehead.

"I haven't seen your place since we helped you move in here," Xavier responded.

He walked further into the living room, and I followed

behind sniffing the roses. He stopped and looked into my eyes and smiled.

"Thanks for the roses."

"You're welcome, Peanut," Xavier answered.

"Let me stop you right there. If we continue this date, you have to stop calling me Peanut. I'm standing before you as a grown woman, with her own mind, complete understanding of what she wants and you sir, are what I desire and want. The real question is if you're ready for me.He stepped closer invaded my space, chest to chest, and my stomach had knots at our closeness. I felt my nerves betraying me, as I looked deep into his eyes. He was one of those rare people with two different colored eyes. Crystal blue on the right and bottle green on the left.

"What's on your mind Chesley?" he asked, already aware of my shortness of breath.

"I've had a bit of a thing for you for the last few years, " I said while looking into his eyes.

That was a big lie. The first time I'd fantasized about Xavier, I couldn't have been much older than fifteen, and he seventeen.

"C'mon, Is this some kind of joke?" he asked, looking a bit surprised at my confession. I know back in high school, he teased me about always following him around, when-ever he came over to our house, along with my brother that I had a crush on him. As I got older I played it off so my brother wouldn't find out.

"No, Xavier," I replied with a quirked eyebrow. "I'm dead serious. I've wanted to fuck you for almost as long as I've known what 'fucking' means."The shock turned into a smile and eventually a little pride. He tightened his grip around my waist, taking the roses out of my hand. He ran a finger on the side of my face from the top of my temple to my bottom lip. Closing my eyes and feeling his thumb run across my lips, I decided to let him know I was serious.

Taking his thumb, I placed it into my mouth; slowly sucking while looking him in the eyes. He furrowed his brow, and his breathing increased.

"You're not making this easy, Baby," He groaned out; licking his lips.

"Nothing about me is easy Xavier, you should know that, and this stays between the two of us," I demanded.

It looked like he was starting to loosen up a bit. I placed a finger on his chest and started tracing it up and down while still sucking on his thumb.

"I won't be some dirty little secret, Chelsey. I'm thirty years old, and your family knows me," He quickly interrupted and stepped back.

"How about we eat and talk first?" I suggested, stepping around him and heading to the dining room table to pick up the bottle of wine.

I bought my house two years ago when I was promoted to Senior Manager of New Accounts at the bank. People figured because I was the daughter of Gerald and Lynidas Hayden, you would think I would automatically have money handed to me. Far from the truth with my parents, I studied and went to school with a degree in Economics and Business. After college, I interviewed for a job at the bank as a teller, and now six years later I'm a Senior Manager.

My house is two stories and around six thousand square feet, with a large backyard and pool. It has large archways, with a bright and airy décor, the sunken tub in the en suite is my favorite. Two people can fit inside snugly. I put up artwork I bought on my trips to Italy and Africa. Above the fireplace hung a family photo of me, Jordan, and my parents in our first holiday picture.

"I'm not down with the games, if you're serious about me, then let them know," Xavier spat as he sat down and smacked my ass, before placing the napkin in his lap.

"Asshole," I mumbled under my breath; sitting down at

the opposite end of the table. He smirked at me, and I felt flutters in my stomach.

"You look beautiful tonight," Xavier said.

"Thank you."

Taking a sip of the wine, Xavier and I made eye contact, and he smiled back at me.

"I've had feelings for you but growing up around your family, I thought I wasn't your type."

"What type is that?" I inquired.

"The regular guy type. Yes, our families know each other. But to tell the truth, if I would have made a move on you in college would you have noticed me?"

"Xavier, I know this is the first time we've actually been able to have this conversation; but I've been in love with you since the first time you protected me against bullies at school. You also let me stay up and watch horror movies when Jordan fell asleep or had a girl in the house while my parents were away," I explained and took another sip of the wine.

His intense eye contact bore into me, and I couldn't turn away. The low music of Crown Royal by Jill Scott playing in the background gave me chills. The quietness and anticipation of what move he's going to make kept me on the edge of my seat.

"Come here," he whispered.

As soon as he said that, I pushed back slowly from the table and stood. Keeping my eyes trained on him, he pushed back from the table and opened his legs. I stood between his thighs and ran my hands up and down his legs; squeezing his dick and feeling his large girth.

"Are you ready for that?" He moaned. He pulled me in closer and placed his hands on my hips, before moving up my back and down to my ass. He squeezed and smacked the right and left cheek.

"Yes," I whispered slowly, running a hand through his

jet-black hair that he kept cut short. Tightening my grip in his hair as he placed kisses on my stomach and continued squeezing my ass.I didn't even have time to start kissing him before he placed his hands under my legs and lifted me up. I giggled like a high school girl, before crossing my legs behind his back and ripping my dress in the process. It was probably a good thing he was much taller than me, even with high heels.

I leaned in to start kissing Xavier, and he instantly responded with an even more intense kiss than I'd given him. I placed a hand on his head, rubbing his short, scruffy hair, before letting it wander down between my legs and down to his crotch. I started rubbing it and felt he was already rock hard.

I got up and led us back to my bedroom, and he placed me down on the bed. He quickly pulled his jacket off and tossed his jacket to the floor, along with his shirt and pants, but left his underwear on. Feeling bold, I looked him in the eyes before tugging them to the floor. His dick pointed right at me, rock hard, just like I'd felt.

"Get on your back," I said, as I stood up to give Xavier a kiss. "I wanna please you."

Xavier did as he was told. He laid down on the bed, and slowly started stroking his dick. I climbed up next to him and leaned down over his crotch. I was thankful for putting my hair up in a bun and out of my way before wrapping my lips around his dick. I started bobbing up and down while keeping eye contact.

"Ughhh...Fuck! Peanut!" Xavier groaned, placing his hands on the back of my head. I smacked his hands away and popped his dick out of my mouth.

"Why'd you stop, shit where did you learn how to suck dick? I thought you were a virgin?" He asked shocked by my oral skills

"I lost my virginity senior year. You and Jordan weren't

stopping anything. No more Peanut tonight; that makes me feel like you only see me as Jordan's little sister," I remarked as I stroked his cock up and down licking the tip.

"God damn it! Sorry Pea...I mean, Baby."

As Xavier's moans grew louder and louder, I realized I hadn't taken my clothes off yet. Popping his cock back out of my mouth, I unzipped my dress, and pulled my thong down.

"Keep the heels on for now," he said.

"Yes, Sir," I replied, as he leaned up off the bed and gripped my chin tight, not hard enough to hurt. His eyes went black, and I knew I should have told him to let me go, but my juices leaked down my leg from his aggressiveness.

"What did you say?"

"I...I... said," I stuttered and looked away from his stare.

"I don't do cookie cutter sex, Chelsey. I like to please my woman with a few toys in the bedroom. Can you handle that?" Xavier asked.

"Yes, Sir," I answered as his lips crashed into mine and we each fervently fought to control the kiss. His tongue invaded mine, and we couldn't keep our hands off each other.

"Good, now it's my turn," Xavier responded, as he picked me up and laid back on the bed with me sitting on his face. The first stroke of his tongue hit my core, and I lost it.

"Xavier!"

He went back and forth with eating me out and spanking my ass and gripping it hard with both hands. I wanted to pull my hair out from the tumultuous mixture of pleasure and pain he was giving me.

"What did I say to call me?"

"Sir! Yes, you're at my spot," I whispered.

"Arghhh...baby, you know what that does to me,"

Xavier groaned, as he continued biting and licking my sweet pussy.

CHAPTER
Four

XAVIER

"GIVE IT TO M-" Chelsey started, but her begging erupted into moans when I quickly slid a finger in her tight asshole. "Fuuuuuuuck!"

"Don't pass out on me now, Chelsey, you're a big girl, right? I thought you could handle this," I taunted as I stroked her.

"Xavier... please. Ohh God, I can't take it anymore," Chelsey groaned and picked up a pillow to cover her screams. I yanked it away and started playing with her clit while pinching her nipples with my other hand.

"Here's what's going to happen, Juicy. From this moment on you belong to me and when I call, you answer; no hiding from your parents or Jordan. We can tell them together if you want, but I refuse to miss out on claiming this pussy every night."

"Okay."

"Good, now it's time to see you squirt."

"I've never squirted before Xavier," She replied.

" God, baby you don't know what that does to me" I said and leaned up to meet her for a kiss.

I grabbed a condom out of my wallet and quickly

sheathed my dick. Even though I've had a lot of sexual partners, I always got tested and used a condom. Each partner I've been with lasted for months or years, I never just hit and ran through women. I did have some common sense from being raised by a single mother.

Chesley leaned back toward the headboard with her legs wide open, rubbing her breasts with one hand and pleasing herself with the other hand. Wanting to find out how kinky she was, I looked in her nightstand; finding what I was looking for.

"How long have you had this bullet?" I asked, turning it on and getting back on the bed to pull her down closer to me. Her eyes bugged out at me finding her little secret.

"Not long, maybe a few months."

"Have you ever been double stuffed baby?" I asked.

Her eyes went wide, and she looked around the room nervously. I wasn't going to fuck her in the ass tonight. I'd save that for another day. I couldn't wait to show her body pleasures she's never had.

"We can save it for another night. I do want to hear you scream my name," I said and thrust into her warm, tight core as deep as I could.

"Ohhhh.... you feel so good, Xavier," She moaned as she gripped the sheets.

My dick was about nine inches, Chelsey would feel it tomorrow. Fortunately, I knew how to use it properly, and hit all the right spots. I knew some women couldn't take a big dick and guys didn't know how to work it, so they both received pleasure. She had nothing to worry about with me.

"Rub my clit, Xavier," Chelsey begged.

Her begging and the facial expressions she wore had me in the stratosphere. This felt like home. I slowed down my pace before placing a thumb on her clit. Chelsey's breathing escalated as I rubbed it intensely. Learning what pleased her sexually, was giving me a high. Her pussy leaked like a faucet, and I could feel her coming close to an orgasm after a few minutes.

I slowed down the pace and pulled out. Chelsey looked pissed with a scrunched-up face. I bent down and kissed her nastily on the mouth and bit her bottom lip.

"Get on your knees," I told her.

Chelsey got down on the floor and stuck her tongue out. I slapped my dick against her tongue once, twice and slid into her warm throat. Closing my eyes, I could feel her hands gripping my dick as she moved up and down hitting the back of her throat.

"Chelsey. I swear you better never do this with anyone else. Fuck baby!"

She giggled, and the vibration went from my spine all the way down to my curling toes.

"You're everything baby," I whispered, running a hand down her cheek.

She sped up her pace and jerked me off at the same time as my cum released in the condom.

"We have to get tested soon because I want to feel all of you," I remarked.

"I'm on birth control, so we don't have to worry about kids anytime soon," Chesley responded.

I helped her to stand up and straddle my lap and grabbed another condom out of my wallet. As soon as it was on, she slid down, and from this angle, her core was strangling my dick.

"I can feel you in my stomach!" Chelsey shouted and bounced up and down on my dick.

Taking her left breast into my mouth, I suckled and tweaked her right nipple like I was a newborn. I reminded myself to talk with Jordan and her parents because keeping us apart wasn't going to happen.

"Slow down," I groaned and captured her lips, I tightened a hand around her neck, not too much, but enough to give her pleasure while bouncing her up and down.

"Shit! I'm cumming!" Chelsey screamed.

Meeting her thrust for thrust, she started shaking as her orgasm rolled through her. I pulled her off my dick, and her juices leaked down. I bit and licked at a fast pace as she shook uncontrollably and played with her clit.

"I think you broke me."

"Baby, that was just the first round," I replied.

She pushed me away as her body was still coming down from her orgasm. I rubbed up and down her body kissing her hip, the palm of her hand and her lips. I wanted her to know this was real.

———

The next morning, I left Chelsey's house after the fourth round of sex and breakfast. Her being the main course. I decided to get the conversation with Jordan over with before we talk with her parents. I'm meeting him at the gym for an early workout since we usually did this before he went to work at the bank. I wasn't expecting him to love the idea of us being together, but he won't be the reason we're not together. Unless Chelsey decided I'm not boyfriend material.

Parking in my usual spot I noticed Jordan's Benz parked already. Grabbing my gym bag, I head inside to my office to prepare myself for what's to come.

"What took you so long? I'm usually the one that's late," Jordan stated from inside my office, sitting in my chair with his legs on top of my desk.

"I had a date, sorry I'm late and get out of my seat," I replied and sat my gym bag down next to the door. Walking around to sit in my chair, Jordan got up and passed the extra coffee over.

"Who with this time? Teresa or Abigail? For a white boy, you get more play than me in these streets," Jordan joked.

I burst out in laughter and slapped hands with him. I felt my phone vibrate so I pulled it out of my pockets checking my messages, I noticed Chelsey sent a photo of her in bed naked wrapped up in the sheets. Nodding my head and biting my lip, I turned it off and put it back in my pocket.

"Did Teresa send you a naked photo? Let me see since one of us is getting laid; I might as well live vicariously through you," Jordan declared.

"Uhh, this isn't from Teresa; as a matter of fact, I need to talk to you about something."

"What's up, you need money? I know you're planning on buying the gym," Jordan inquired.

"No man, the process for the gym is going great. Thanks again for signing off on the loan. I appreciate your support," I explained.

"Okay, this sounds like you're dying. You need a kidney or something?" Jordan joked, placing his coffee down on the desk.

"I'm dating your sister!" I blurted out.

He busted out laughing, and I stood up, walked around, and shut the door.

"I'm serious, Jordan, we're dating. I've had a crush on her since high school."

"Xavier, you're the biggest man-whore, even more so than I was and you're trying to tell me you decided to settle down and date my sister?" Jordan inquired as he picked up his coffee taking a tentative sip.

"She's everything I want in a woman. I'd like your blessing before things get serious."

"All I'm going to say is cut off the other women you're dating before you get serious with her. Chelsey's an adult, but she's still my little sister, and if you hurt her, you already know what I'm capable of doing."

"I don't plan on hurting her, eventually, down the road, I can see her as my wife."

"You're serious about this?" Jordan asked rubbing his chin as he contemplated the idea.

My phone vibrated on the desk; I saw a text from Chelsey asking if I wanted to meet her for dinner tonight.

Chelsey: Dinner my place or yours?

Me: I'm working late tonight, baby.

Chelsey: :(

Me: If I get done early, I'll grab something for us.

"That has to be Chelsey; I've never seen a smile on your face that big before."

I nod and place my phone back down on the desk to continue checking emails and scheduling more clients.

"So, you're stopping being a playboy. I was going to live through you dating multiple women since I'm getting married and one day having kids."

"Yep, and Chelsey already knows about my past and family drama. She doesn't care."

"All I can say is get ready to tell my father. My mom doesn't care as much as my father does with how it'll be portrayed in the media."

"I figured he would have a problem, but hopefully when he sees how Chelsey is treated, he will be fine with us dating. I mean he was the one that let me spend the night at your home whenever my parents got into it and divorced," I replied.

"That's different in his eyes; you're dating his little girl. He has high expectations of who she should be with and marry," Jordan said as he stood up to shake hands and leave.

"I'll see you tomorrow night for game night at Broderick's," I said.

CHAPTER

Five

CHELSEY

HE RUBBED and pulled some moisture out with his fingers and motioned for me to open my mouth a little as I breathed even harder, grabbing his other arm with a firm grip as my back began to arch. Xavier pushed his thumb a little harder and kept it moving around, trying to ensure he didn't lose the spot while simultaneously fingering me.

I responded, moaning a little. "Yes, Xavier, fuck!" He kept his pace, tightening a grip around my ankle that was hovering over his shoulder, as he focused all his concentration on pleasuring me.

"You're all mine," Xavier groaned, kissing behind my ear. I felt so overheated with his large body engulfing me, but the fullness of his girth was enough for me to want to keep him locked away.

"I'm about to cum!"

"Not yet," He said, abruptly pulling out leaving me shocked and frustrated. He ran his fingers down my body while holding me closely from behind and gently kissed down the side of my neck under my earlobe. I moved my head to the side, giving him more of my neck to kiss, and brought up my right arm to cup around his head, my fingers ran through his hair. His kisses were gentle as he began to remove my black lace panties, I leaned up to help him unclasp my bra. I turned to face him and pushed my tongue into his mouth; our lips consuming as he pounded into me.

"I love you, Chelsey, do you hear me?" He grunted, smacking my thigh, and then rubbing the sting away.

"I love you too, Xavier! Fuck, keep going, almost there." I screamed, juices leaking out onto my new sheets.

"Arghhh!" We both climaxed at the same time.

———

Two hours later we sat in my parents' home, waiting for my father to get off a business call. My brother and I talked, and he's calmed down from the initial shock of finding out we're dating.

"So, Chelsey, what's so important that you needed to have everyone here for a special dinner?" Dad asked, placing his cell phone down on the table, and kissing my mother on the cheek.

"I have an announcement, and I wanted to let you and Mom know before the public gets wind of it," I replied calmly, taking a sip of my water.

Everyone stopped eating and looked at Jordan and then me. I felt all eyes were waiting for the bomb to drop. Gripping Xavier's hand, I placed it on the table, and my parents' eyes narrowed as we smiled at each other.

"Xavier and I are dating," I stated in a calm voice.

"When did this happen, Chelsey?" Mom asked, surprised at my statement looking between the both of us.Feeling the tension in the air, Jordan didn't make it any better as he kept eating and ignored my father's glare.

"Did you know about this, Jordan?" Dad questioned, gesturing with his fork between Xavier and me.

"Dad, I'm a grown woman. I don't need Jordan to know everything about my love life. Besides, you've known Xavier since he was a kid. What's the problem?"

"Listen, Mr. and Mrs. Hayden, I care about Chelsey a great deal, and have nothing but the utmost respect for her," Xavier said.

"Xavier, I'm not sure what Chelsey has told you. But she doesn't have the best track record with dating. Too many times we've had to step in when she's dated someone questionable."

I was pissed off at the mention of past mistakes with the guys I dated. I didn't want Xavier feeling uncomfortable because my father pushed his agenda on who I should date.

"Pop, calm down. Xavier filled me in on him dating Chelsey already. He's a solid guy and buying his own business with the fitness studio," Jordan responded.

"Am I the only one that sees this as a mistake? Chelsey, you and Xavier come from different worlds. I'm sorry, but you're not dating him!" Dad demanded, stood up and walked out of the room; leaving everyone shocked at his response. Trying to salvage what was left of dinner, Jordan told a funny joke about him and Emma going out to the lake and getting lost. Thinking that would smooth over the tension in the room. We all knew how Dad could get if things didn't go his way. Lily brought over more wine and dessert and we started talking about Xavier's new plans for the gym. Ideas like opening a second location if everything takes off.

"Are you happy Chelsey?" Mom questioned, eating a bite of the cheesecake Lily made. I nodded my head in answer and turn toward Xavier placing a kiss on his lips.

"Very much so, and Xavier's not going anywhere and hopefully Dad will come around." I answered and stood up, walked toward my mother to give her a kiss goodnight as Xavier shook hands with my brother and we went home.

———

Two hours later, I finished talking to my mom on the phone. She apologized for my dad walking out on dinner and let me know she's happy that I found someone that cares for me so deeply. Xavier has done nothing but make me smile throughout our short time together. Xavier continued rubbing my feet as we sat on his couch inside his condo.

"What did she say?" Xavier asked, kissing the sole of my feet.

"She apologized for his behavior; and said give it time. I have my own place and a job; I shouldn't feel like I must live by his rules. I love my father, but sometimes he makes it hard to be his child with his impossible standards of what a Hayden is supposed to be." I answered, as I removed myself from his hold and kissed him on the lips.

"How about I cook you something to eat and then watch a movie. My first appointment isn't until nine tomorrow," Xavier replied, standing to help me up off the couch.

"I'm tired, can you take me to bed instead? I'll talk to my father alone before we get to a place we can't come back from."

I followed behind him as he turned the light off in the kitchen and living room and we headed to his bedroom. For a bachelor, his bedroom was neat and modern with cream and white bedding. A king size bed sat against one wall with a TV across from it. Paintings from local artists adorned the walls. Plopping down on his bed, he stood in front of me to help take my clothes off. He passed me a t-shirt and shorts to sleep in since I forgot to bring anything with me after we left my parents' home.

CHAPTER

Six

XAVIER

THE ANNUAL CARD night at Broderick's house was the usual thing with strippers dancing, a bartender sending endless shots to our table and Jordan losing money left and right.

"I fold, fuck!" Jordan shouted and threw his cards down.

Laughing at the expression on Jordan's face, I took a shot from the waitress and placed another bet.

"So, Xavier, how's it going with buying the fitness studio?" Broderick asked, shuffling the cards.

"I signed the papers last week; just waiting on few things. Old man George is excited to finally retire and leave the building to me."

"Nice, I have a few clients looking to join; let me know when they can come in for a consultation. Did I mention they're both hot with a large ass and tits?" Broderick joked, smacking a girl on the butt as she walked by.

"I'm good on the dating front," I responded.

"Ohhhh!" Everyone at the table replied at the same time.

"Don't tell me Xavier Hardy has finally settled down with one woman," Broderick said.

"I have, and she's the best thing that has ever happened to me," I answered, slamming the shot glass of whiskey down. I replayed in my mind the night before with Chesley, legs spread wide as my head was buried between her legs as I ate her sweet pussy.

"How's the pussy?" Broderick questioned.

"Alright, change the subject," Jordan responded.

"What, it has to be the best pussy and head in the world to make him monogamous," Broderick remarked.

Jordan looked at Broderick with a scowl on his face ready to beat his ass for talking about Chelsey.

"I'm dating Chelsey, man," I said, getting up to grab another beer.

A stripper came over and sat in Jordan's lap, she placed a cigar between his lips and lit it.

"Chelsey, little Peanut, his sister?" Broderick asked, pointing at Jordan.

"Leave my sister out of this conversation," Jordan stated.

"Wait a minute, you're busting down thick ass Chelsey? Damn, if I knew she was up for dating, I would have given her a shot," Broderick joked.

"I suggest you keep your thoughts about anything pertaining to Chelsey to yourself. I'd hate to have to kick your ass in your own home," I demanded, smacking him on the back of the head and sitting back down in my chair.

"Somebody gets testy when Chelsey's name comes up. Sorry, bro. We'll keep our thoughts to ourselves," Broderick responded, as he kissed one of the waitresses on the cheek. Standing up, he took her by the hand, to lead her upstairs to the bedroom.

Most of his parties left us with a choice of picking up a woman and taking her to bed and having all our wildest dreams come to life. But tonight, was the last time of me coming to game night, and I could see Jordan not wanting to be here anymore than I was.

"Are you ready to take off? I need to go talk with your father before I see Chelsey."

"So, my Pop still hasn't given you his blessing?" Jordan asked as we walked out of the house toward our cars to leave.

Getting inside, I put the key in the ignition and rolled the window down. "If I can handle my parents fighting and divorcing, I can handle your father not approving of us dating. It won't stop anything between us; she knows I love her." I answered and started the car, honked my horn and pulled off.

Thirty minutes later, I pulled up at the home of Chelsey's parents. Knocking on the door, I waited for someone to answer.

"Xavier, what are you doing here?" Lily the house-keeper asked.

"How are you, Lily? I came to talk to Gerald if he's home," I replied.

She opened the door, and I walked inside and waited. She motioned at me, and we walked to his office. I knocked and waited for him to respond.

"It's open!" Gerald shouted and waved for me to take a seat in front of his desk.

"How are you, Mr. Hayden?" I asked.

Tossing paperwork inside his desk, Gerald stood and walked around to his bar and poured himself a drink and offered me a drink. Still feeling the effects of drinking at Broderick's house I motioned I was fine.

"Son, I know why you're here, and I have to tell you my mind hasn't changed. Chelsey needs to date someone that has the same pedigree as our family. We run in different circles, and I expect Chelsey to live up to what I've envisioned for her future husband."

"Even if it means she's not happy? Because if you keep pushing your ideas on what and who she should be, you'll end up losing her altogether."

"I can promise Chelsey will never disobey me. In time, she will understand. Have you spoken with your parents lately?" Gerald inquired and sat back down at this desk.

"I don't keep up with my father, Mom is doing great though, and she sends her love."

"Sounds like he's still up to his old tricks of gambling, and we both know with your father having his hands in 'illegal activities', I don't want my daughter around anyone that can get hurt with him around." Gerald said.

Getting upset at the mention of my father's name in the same sentence as Chelsey's was pissing me off. I haven't talked to my father in over a year, and he has nothing to do with Chelsey and me.

"We can agree on that fact Mr. Hayden; my father has nothing to do with what's going on in my life. Soon Chelsey will meet my mom, and hopefully, we can have your blessing. I can promise you I'll always put your daughter first; I'm not leaving her and breaking her heart because you think I'm not the standard you expect a man to be when dating Chelsey. I have my own business now; I'm not rich, but I can take care of her. We both know Chelsey is independent and has her own mind; she doesn't need any man to take care of her."

I reached over to shake his hand as I made eye contact and he nodded and shook my hand. Taking this as a sign that we understand each other, I left to surprise Chelsey at home.

Twenty minutes later, I pulled into her driveway. I shut off my car and grabbed the flowers to take inside. I put the key inside the door and walked inside to the smell of food cooking and low music playing.

"I wasn't expecting you until later tonight," Chelsey said walking over to hug and kiss me.

"These are for you."

"Thanks, baby, how was game night?" Chelsey asked, taking the flowers into the kitchen and placing them into a vase filled with water.

"It was uneventful; I was ready to get back to you."

"Xavier, it's me you're talking to; we both know how those parties go and you just left without attempting to do anything?" Chelsey said, her arched brow furrowed in a questioning manner.

"You're the only one that can please me and besides I needed to talk with your father about us," I replied.

"How did that conversation go?" She leaned in closer and wrapped her arms around my neck. I pulled her in tighter and squeezed her ass.

"It went as expected; he wants you dating guys with money and security. I told him that we're not breaking up and hopefully, we can coexist because I'd hate for him to miss out on your life."

We sat down at the dinner table and continued talking about our issues with both our parents. Chelsey gripped my hand and squeezed while giving me a disappointed look at the mention of her father not budging on us being together.

"Things will work out over time, Peanut," I joked to lighten the mood.

"How is the construction on the gym going?"

"We're about two-thirds finished. I need to upgrade a few pieces of equipment, and then we'll be set to go for an official opening. I can't wait to christen the equipment with you underneath me screaming my name with my dick inside you."

"As long as you let me ride your face first while I do downward dog," Chelsey joked.

"Babe, don't forget we have dinner plans with my mom tomorrow," I reminded Chelsey as she picked up our plates to take them into the kitchen. I grabbed our wine glasses and helped to clean up the kitchen.

"I didn't forget; I was going to ask you what I should wear. She hasn't seen me as your girlfriend only as Jordan's little sister. Should I bring her a gift or something?" Chelsey asked.

Chelsey washed the dishes as I dried, and we walked into her bedroom to get comfortable. Not up to playing tonight, only holding Chelsey in my arms would soothe my frustrations.

"I'm hopping in the shower; would you like to join me?" Chelsey asked, taking her shirt and bra off, and letting it fall to the ground. My dick hardened and poked through my pants at Chelsey standing in front of me holding her breasts. Keeping to my word, I wasn't going to give in to my desires tonight. We both had a long day.

"You go first; I'll only be a distraction for you."

"If you say so," Chelsey responded cheekily, as she leaned down and kissed my lips.

WE WALKED into the bedroom after leaving a trail of our clothes on the stairs. A few minutes later Xavier spread my ass cheeks apart before sliding in yet again. He was a bit more gentle than before, putting more effort into each thrust instead of just going as fast as he could. My back arched as I tried to tighten my grip on the headboard. The smacking of skin and hearing his moans in my ear sent me catapulting over the edge.

"Fuck, that's good," I moaned.

"God damn," he panted. "You're so tight, baby."

Xavier ran a hand around to my chest, tweaking each nipple. He fumbled to flick my clit, as his thrusts were steady, hovering with his chest to my back, heavy breathing in my ear. He wrapped his arm around my midriff, instead coming between my legs from the front. The very moment Xavier touched my clit, a deep sigh of relief poured through. It seemed to make him understand he'd found it, because he started rubbing it just as fast as before.

"What time do we have to be at your mother's for dinner?" I inquired, moaning, meeting him thrust for thrust.

"Shit! We might be missing dinner," Xavier replied, starting to pick up his pace again. His hips were smashing against my ass with each thrust, making a "slap" sound echo across the room. I prayed to God that I don't end up walking funny before meeting his mother on our official dinner as a couple.

I didn't have time to finish my thought before wave after wave of pleasure started flooding my senses. I had gotten caught up in thinking, and hadn't not ced the fact that I was just about to cum. I felt myself losing balance as Xavier started thrusting a little softer.

If I were to guess, I probably let out one constant moan during my orgasm - but there was no way for me to know for sure, since everything around us disappeared when hc came spurting ropes of cum in my ass. With sweat dripping down our bodies, Xavier slapped my ass, quite hard and let out a loud "fuck" before placing a gentle hand on the back of my neck. He turned me toward him before devouring my lips, taking dominance over the kiss.

"How about I run us a bath and make us a quick dinner because I'm not letting this sweet ass out of my sight?" Xavier asked, getting out of bed and walking to the bathroom. Hearing the water run, he turns it back off and comes back to wipe between my legs and kiss me on the forehead.

"I don't want your mother hating me and thinking I canceled dinner tonight. Bad enough my parents are barely talking to us," I responded, lying down in his arms trying to catch my breath.

"I promise Chelsey; my mom loves you. We can only control what happens in this relationship. Doesn't matter what my parents, yours, or society has to say. Nothing is tearing us apart. I can't promise the luxury lifestyle of having maids, and fancy parties to go to, but I can promise to take care of your heart, mind, and give you multiple orgasms at least five times a day," He joked, tightening a grip around my waist lifting me. I wrapped my legs around him as he carried me into the bathroom.

"When you look at it that way, missing one dinner won't hurt," I responded as I ran my tongue across his bottom lip biting and soothing the sting with a kiss.

Reader Questions

Reader Questions: Email responses to info@ 304publishing.com

1. What nickname was Chelsey called when she was younger?

2. Who did Chelsey set her brother up on a date with?

3. What do you think Xavier's father is into?

4. What was Chelsey wearing on her first date with Xavier?

5. What business did Xavier buy?

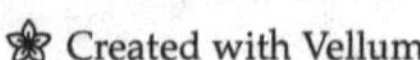

PART

Two

Synopsis

EVERY TIME WE TOUCH

XAVIER FINALLY PROCLAIMED his love for his best friend's sister.

Chelsey finally announced her love for her brother's best friend.

Every time they touch the passion is explosive, love is sweet, and the protection he gives is nurturing.

But will this sweet connection be enough?

As they navigate this new relationship, temptation draws them into a spotlight neither dared to explore on their own.

Note: Xavier and Chelsey were first introduced in "Wet Heat" a novella -A Steamy friends to lovers. This is a short novelette to update on the couple that helps to introduce a new series coming out in 2020. This must be read in order to understand context. Deals with explicit sex scenes, adult content and leaves off with a cliffhanger.

CHAPTER

Eight

CHELSEY

THE LOW HUM OF D'ANGELO'S song "Lady" is playing in the background as Xavier massages my feet. We never made it to his mother's house for dinner, something in his eyes, that hunger and uninhibited urge to devour my entire soul and make me his, was something neither of us could resist. We both lie naked in bed, blankets strewn out all around us, pillows on the floor. The smell of sex is in the air, with the air conditioner blasting low, lights softly glowing, and our bodies slowly coming down from another explosive orgasm. It's rare for us to only go three rounds in one night unless we're both exhausted from work. Tonight though, I could tell something was on his mind, and sex wasn't the answer to all our problems. He's always challenging me to be honest with him, even if it hurts. It's time for him to do the same. I have to cut the silence in the room. "Why are you so quiet?" I lean over and press my lips to his thigh as he rubs a hand over my cheek.

He smiles and bends down to kiss my lips. "Reminding myself how lucky I am that you're in my life."

I grab his cheek, holding him in place to prolong our kiss.

"Baby, you're bad for me. We've already had sex three times, and you better cut it out before I have you on your back again, screaming my name during round four." Xavier stated with a low chuckle.

I lifted my leg off his lap and spread them wide. Taking my middle and index finger, I opened my pussy lips for him to see what he's been craving.

I'm already leaking, and he grins, leaning over and bending down, wrapping his arm around my midriff to keep me still. I caressed the back of his neck as we meet once again with longing, knowing, and ardent desire. The cool brush of hands rubbing up and down my stomach drives me wild. Xavier's the type of man that shows every inch, dimple, roll, or imperfection attention to let me know it all belongs to him. Of course I've had my moments of doubt, based on his past girlfriends looking like supermodels. But not once has he ever made me feel inadequate. Nor has he allowed anyone else to state I wasn't the typical person he dated.

His tongue explores the softness of my lower lips, gently teasing, taking my bud into his mouth, biting my inner thigh, and then kissing the sting away.

"Mmm... sweet!" Xavier mumbles under his breath.

"Yes."

"Do you understand what you do to me, baby?"

I can barely concentrate as my eyes slide closed in ecstasy. Answering Xavier's question is the last thing I want to do. He grabs my hand, tugging it over and licking each finger and sticking them into my pussy. As his tongue continues to play with my bud, he slips a hand down to rub my clit. I stare into his eyes, and now he takes hold of his hard dick, gliding his hand up and down his shaft as he watches the scene unfold before him.

"Fuck! Keep going, baby."

"Xavier, shit! Please fuck me now," I cry out, keeping the

same pace as him with our mutual masturbating. He moans softly as his lips trace a sensuous path up my stomach to my nipples, never letting go of his dick. I squirm beneath him as his hard body hovers over me, his sweat dripping onto my skin.

"You look so fucking beautiful, come for me, baby," Xavier commands, kissing each nipple, his other hand lifting my right breast, and he desperately takes it into his mouth like a starving baby. An electric shock shoots through my body as his raw sensuousness carries me to greater heights.

"Goddamit!" Xavier says, squirting on my stomach and thigh.

"Ahh! Baby, I'm coming."

A few seconds later, my orgasm crashes into me as Xavier clenches me tighter in his arms. Tenderly raining kisses down my check, and across my shoulder as our trembling subsides. He eases out of my core and pats my thigh, winking as he stands up and strides out of the room, heading in the direction of the bathroom to grab a wet towel to wipe his semen off. I lick a little off my stomach to show him it doesn't matter to me that he came early.

"Are you ready to talk now?" I ask, getting out of bed to grab my robe so we can talk.

Xavier comes over, towel still in hand, and pulls me into his chest and we stay silent for a few minutes.

"I want this to be forever, not just girlfriend and boyfriend. My future includes you Chelsey. And I know you've gotten things calmed down with your dad. My mom will love you for sure, but I need to know that when I ask your parents for your hand in marriage, it won't be a one-sided feeling. I want to know that you want it too," Xavier explains interlocking our hands.

"I love you, Xavier, always have, but don't you think it's a little early for marriage?"

Shaking his head, he tenderly pecks my lips and then my forehead. "Baby, I never thought we'd be here together. For so long, I wished that we would have taken that step into a relationship earlier rather than now. But love has no time limit."

He sighs, running a hand down his face and looking toward the ceiling. "I'm not saying we get married tomorrow, but I'm at a point in my life that I want the wife, two-point three kids, and a home. The constant back and forth to each other's apartments can only satisfy me for so long. I need you morning, noon, and night Chelsey. And if that's going to be a problem, then we need to rethink things."

"I want that too baby. How about we take a bubble bath and get some rest. Tomorrow we can talk some more about our future over breakfast," I answer, pulling him in closer for a kiss and reaching for his hand.

He grasped my hand tight, bringing it to his lips and placing a kiss on the palm and knuckles as we walked toward the bathroom to clean up.

CHAPTER

Nine

CHELSEY

XAVIER WAS STILL ASLEEP when I left for work this morning, so I hoped to talk about the next step in our relationship after our date tonight. We've let too much time go by between us to not be honest with where things are heading in the future. I turned my phone on vibrate before replying to his good morning message.

Xavier: Good morning beautiful.

Me: Thanks Handsome.

We have a big client coming in today that I didn't even get a chance to prepare for because my father told me about 10 minutes before the client was due to arrive. As the branch manager, it's my job to handle high profile clients, but I often pass them off to my other managers seeing as though they need the practice, but I'm always available if something happens and a little more finesse is needed. But he insisted that I handle this one personally, as the less people that know about the client at our bank the better.

Xavier texts me again to have a good day, and I reply right as someone taps on my door.

"Come in!" I shout.

"Chelsey, your ten o'clock appointment is here to see

you. Do you mind if security comes in and checks your office over? It's protocol," Alisha, my new secretary asked.

"Sure, but I doubt you'll find anyone hiding in here ready to harm our client seeing as I've been in my office all alone today," I reply, standing up as two large men with badges and wearing suits walk into the room. One announced into his earpiece that the place was clear and waved for someone to step inside.

My mouth hangs open as the current Democratic senator of the state of Tennessee walks inside my office.

She's even more beautiful in person.

She reaches out to shake my hand, and I grasp hers gently, not wanting to seem over-eager. Amongst my idols, besides Beyonce, was Senator Maya Hill.

Her presence commands the room, and it isn't only because of her beauty. This woman is smart, funny, sarcastic, and stern. Most of my family and friends don't understand that I'm more of an independent thinker when it comes to politics, I'm not a staunch Republican or Democrat rather I pay attention to what they're doing in the community to make our lives better, especially for those that have less than my family. Listening to some of the debates, Maya helped to inspire me to keep an eye on what politicians are doing in Congress. I clear my throat and wave for her to take a seat in the chair in front of my desk.

"Senator Hill, you'll have to forgive me. When my father said we'd have a VIP client coming in this morning he didn't say it would be you," I tell her.

"Please, call me Maya," Senator Hill replies and turns to her bodyguards, gesturing for them to leave the room.

"Oh, okay, Maya, how can we help you today?"

Maya opens her purse and pulls out a thick yellow envelope. "Chelsey, you don't mind if I call you Chelsey, do you?"

"Of course not. Go ahead."

"I need to keep something safe. A friend told me this was the best bank in the state, and that I could trust you implicitly," Maya answers, sliding the envelope across my desk.

"What's inside, if you don't mind me asking?"

"I would prefer not to answer that. Sorry, it's regarding a personal matter. I would also like to make a deposit along with opening a safe-deposit box. I want to deposit five million dollars. For my niece and nephew's college fund." Maya states firmly, pulling out her checkbook and ID.

"Uhmm, okay, as long as it's nothing illegal I guess we can keep it in a safe deposit box. How many people will have access?" I begin pulling up the necessary paperwork.

"Just you and me," Maya answers succinctly, taking the receipt from the deposit. She stands and takes a business card out of her purse. I pick mine up from off my desk, and we exchange numbers.

"We should have lunch sometime. I think you'd fit right in with my friends," Maya says, walking toward the door as I follow behind her to where the safety deposit boxes located in the vault. As we leave, her bodyguards trail behind without a smile or a smirk across their faces. "This must be what Meghan Markle and Prince Harry deal with?" I blurted out hoping to get a response and fell flat with my joke.

Maya, smiled politely in that mannerism of wanting to say something like "Girl, you aren't Eddie Murphy, so keep the jokes to the professionals" But with her being in the political arena she has to keep up appearances.

A part of me feels a little uncomfortable keeping something hidden in our bank vaults without knowing what it is, but I figure my father promised absolute discretion throughout the process, and we aim to please.

"Okay so here's your key, Maya, and your box number is

four-fourteen-nine. If you ever have any problems with the box we can change it for you free of charge."

"Thanks, Chelsey, I'm not planning on coming in and out frequently. With me heading to the office early, and this being a sensitive matter, I couldn't put it off any longer. I thought this would be a perfect time, and your father speaks highly of your discretion for high profile clients at your branch," Maya answers.

"I have to admit I was completely caught off guard when you walked inside, I was expecting an actor or singer. My father kept this visit a closely guarded secret. I guess because I'm a massive fan of yours."

"Well that makes two of us, I love seeing strong women in charge and running things. We have to do lunch some time. Don't be a stranger," Maya says with a smile, walking out of the bank with her security flanking her.

CHAPTER

Ten

XAVIER

I SIT THE TEN-POUND weights down on the stand and pick up my phone to return a text to Chelsey about making dinner early.

Chesley: Babe, I need to stop by my parents' house after work.

Me: No problem, babe, I'll meet you around eight at Dominique's.

Chelsey: Sounds good.

Me: Wear that red dress you wore on our first date.

Chesley: Why? It never stays on long enough.

Me: I know, I want to have dessert before dinner.

Chesley: You know this will have my panties wet all day when you talk like that.

Me: That's the point, baby.

"Man, what are you doing tonight? Emma wants you and Chelsey to come out with us tonight to visit this new club," Jordan wondered, bending down moving the weights on and off the barbell stand to get the correct ratio.

Closing out my messages, I place my phone in the front pocket of my shorts.

"We're going out for dinner after she meets with your

parents tonight. What's this club about?" I question. Chelsey and I are more homebodies, and we don't need all the glam and nightlife, being surrounded by crowds of people. The two of us alone watching TV or hanging out at the beach satisfied us more.

"Someplace Emma found and wants to try out before that baby belly starts showing. I want to keep my baby happy, so I agreed and told her don't be out here showing off all my goodies," Jordan states, leaning down on the weight bench.

I walk over to spot him with switching out the ten pound weights with twenty-five.

"You don't know anything about the club? Where is it located? Who owns it?"

"You know Emma—damn...one... two... shit... I'm getting old—is always in somebody's business, and I guess her group of girlfriends told her about this place that's exclusive. You have to be invited or referred just to get in. Something I'm not in the mood for. But if she's happy, then I am. I'm trying to be more open to her feelings after our last blow up. Besides, my parents are blowing me up constantly about us getting married, and that's something I know I can't see myself doing at my age." Jordan replied, pushing the weights up above his head and counting to thirty.

"You know your sister and I aren't usually club goers. I'll ask her before I leave work today," I answer, helping him to elevate his arms above his head.

"That's true, but I figured Emma could talk her into going. As her best friend, she wouldn't want to disappoint her. If it came from me, you know she'd say hell no. Anyway, what's up with you two lovebirds? Honestly, I'm still in shock you're still together. After so many years of being around each other as friends growing up and you having the reputation of being the playboy up until just a few months ago.."

"Why? Because she's your sister or because I'm a 'reformed whore,' as you like to state to our friends?" I chortle, bending down to grab the bottle of water and passing it over to him.

He nods in agreement, laughing. "Hell yeah, you both played me all this time thinking your ass was looking out for my sister and next thing I know you're dating and shit. My sister has dealt with a lot of assholes. Hell, I'm an asshole when it comes to dating, so I know she can do better than picking guys like me. Emma was the one to tame me, so it's weird seeing that she tamed and calmed you down."

We switch out, and I lean back. He spots me this time. "We grew up around each other, and I can't say that didn't affect my decisions. Plus, Chelsey's always been someone I wanted to protect. Yeah, she's Peanut, but at some point, I started seeing her as my woman and holding those feelings in for so long caused them to come rushing to the surface. When she approached me, I had to ask if this was something she wanted for real, because I knew I couldn't turn my feelings off if we started up."

"I give you credit for standing up to my dad. If that was me, I wouldn't even care if the father didn't like me. Anyway, how are things going with you two? My sister hasn't called me crying, so I guess you're handling your business and taking care of her. Otherwise, I'd have to kick your ass," Jordan jokes, rubbing his hands together in anticipation.

I blow him off and pick the weights up again. "One...two...three...you could never beat me up in high school. Everybody was shocked; this white boy has hands. Besides, you know Chelsey is my Queen. I would take a bullet for her in a heartbeat." I respond, continuing to count up to thirty.

"That's true, remember the time you almost got jumped

by those dudes that were looking for your dad because he owed them money?"

Feeling my blood boil at the mention of my father, I change the subject to keep my mood in a better place.

"Did Emma tell you what time the club opens tonight?" I question, as I put the weights back on the stand, and stand up.

Jordan throws me a towel, and we walk off toward my office.

"She only said dress in a suit and tie. I pray it's not a snooty, rich, uptight club. I love making money as much as the next man, but I need a break from the pretentious assholes sometimes," Jordan says and sits down on the couch in my office. I head to my desk and place my phone on charge, turning the computer on to check for any new emails.

"Did she give you a name?" I inquire.

"Something called Seeking; I'll have to ask her when I get home. I wasn't planning on going to the office today, and she's out shopping for dresses to wear for tonight."

"Seeking, huh... that's a weird name for a club," I mutter. I type it in Google. The only thing that pops up is an outdated website called "Seeking Pleasure", so I close out of the link and decide to call Chelsey and see if she wants to go. Jordan stands to stretch. He heads toward the bathroom in my office as I wait for Chelsey to answer the phone.

Eleven

XAVIER

"HELLO," CHELSEY ANSWERS, sounding out of breath.

Hearing rustling on the other end makes me feel suddenly possessive.

"Where are you?"

"Hey baby, I'm hanging with Emma for lunch. Why do you sound pissed off? What are you doing?" she asks quizzically.

I let out a relieved breath. "Nothing, I was curious about this club thing that Emma and Jordan want us to go to tonight, have you ever heard of it?" I ask as I hear water running and Jordan walking back out. He motions he's leaving and I nod coolly.

"No, but Emma said the place is ultra exclusive, and we'd like it from what she's heard. I think it'd been fun to get out and explore new things. We've been stuck in the house for the past few days and meeting new people can't hurt." Chelsey starts mumbling to someone about upgrading her fries to large and getting a lemonade to drink.

"Jordan just left. He told me about this place. I tried researching it online, and nothing came up. We can go have dinner and then meet up with them and go to the club afterward if you want. Are you going to your parents' place early?"

"Yep. My father asked for me to come over and talk about the meeting I had with our new client this morning. I told him it went fine, but you know Dad. Even though I'm the manager, he still needs to have a hand in the day to day operations."

I can tell she's frustrated. Mr. Hayden lets other people run things to a certain extent, but he'll always let you know it's his name behind any major deals. "Do you need me there with you? Your father and I have an understanding now, and he knows I'm not going anywhere after our last conversation." I suggest, trying to help ease her worries.

"I can handle him. Jordan and my mom both told him to back off a little and let me run things my way. At some point, the realization that I'm not a little girl anymore will wake him up to the idea that I don't need his permission. Let's talk about us and how I miss your lips, touch, and... Emma wouldn't this dress be cute on me tonight?" Chelsey gets distracted easily when she's out shopping.

But her voice alone has my dick rising. "Chelsey..." I groan trying to calm my dick down before someone walks into my office.

"Sorry baby, I saw this beautiful light green dress in a store window and got distracted. I know you wanted me to wear the red dress from our first date, but this would have you not letting me out of the house with the way it would caress my curves. Emma walked off to the bathroom, so we have a few minutes to talk privately."

"Instead of going out tonight, how about you buy the dress and wear it for me inside the house and I devour your pretty pussy. You can wear those six-inch heels and your hair down, and that perfume I love so much," I replied, suddenly not caring about going out anymore.

"That does sound like an intriguing proposition, but I promised Emma we'd go tonight."

"Can you stop by the gym on your way to your parents' house?" I asked, needing to be inside her now.

"You're such a bad influence Xavier. Let me buy this dress and I'll push my other meetings back and head over to you before I meet up with my parents." Chelsey giggles as she hangs up, I could hear Emma whispering something in her ear.

———

ONE HOUR LATER, I HAVE the door to my office locked and Chelsey on top of my desk with her legs wide open and my face planted between her thighs.

"Ughh, mhmm... Xavier! Please." Chelsey mutters in a low moan as my tongue glides in and out of her pussy, my finger poking her tight asshole. The double combination always has her leaking quickly.

Lapping up her juices, and her sweet moans, arouses me even more and has my dick rising in my pants. We don't have much time with her needing to meet up with her father, and then our dinner plans tonight. My gaze stays riveted on her face, and now moves over her body slowly. Something intense flares in me. Other men will be looking at her in the new green dress she's showing off. It's a tight fitted dress with a long split on both sides up to her thighs. The bust curves across her stomach and is held up with thin straps.

At first, I wanted to protest and put up a fight, but she distracted me with a gorgeous smile and sweet kisses. Chelsey unlocks my heart and soul with her love. She gives me unconditional love and support even though she could be with any man that has the same status as her family. She loves me as I am. Honestly, growing up around her and seeing her only as a friend was the best thing for our relationship, even though I wanted to kick any guy's ass that stepped to her face. Since the moment we met I felt a connection, one that went far beyond just sex, we understood each other and cared for the same things and reached for more than what was expected of us based on our family's pressure. I'll never let her go. Since finding out she's held the same feelings, and knowing we want a future together, I don't see my future without her standing next to me.

"Baby! Mmmm. Fuck, let me up." Chelsey moans trying to push my head away.

I shake my head no, smiling and send her back to arching up off the desk, not able to handle my oral skills once again. My stomach tingles. I need to be inside her before I come too early like a fifteen year old boy who's having sex for the first time.

"You think you're slick, huh," Chelsey says and finally pushes me away, slowly moving off the desk and sinks down to her knees in front of me, pulling my shorts down as she goes.

CHAPTER

Twelve

CHELSEY

XAVIER IS THE BEST lover I've ever had. And while my friends sometimes complain about how their boyfriends never put them first in the bedroom, I've never had that problem. I refuse to spill all of our bedroom secrets, but I'd say without a doubt he takes excellent care of me. He always makes sure to put me first in everything we do. Like right now, before I could get a word out, he'd put me on top of his desk and spread me open after seeing the dress I'd got from the mall for our date tonight.

"That's right, Pe...I mean, baby." He stutters in a low groan as my tongue licks the tip of his dick. I squat in front of him with my other hand playing with my pussy as we stare into each other's eyes.

I know it was hard for him to get over calling me by my childhood nickname, but at some point, he had to see me as the woman I had become. I'm no longer just the little girl tagging along behind him and my brother.

"Tell me how you feel baby?" I tease; taking his entire dick down, letting it hit the back of my throat and now popping it out of my mouth. I take my other hand out of my pussy and smear some of my juices on his cock.

"Baby, you just started something you can't finish," he says with a guttural groan.

He tries to reach and pull me up, and I slap his hands away. "No, it's my turn now." I told him, fondling his balls and lifting his dick, gently biting and licking both. He stokes a smoothly growing fire inside of me that violently ignites whenever our bodies become one through sex.

"Aghh, shit...hold up Chelsey. Damn it! I'm going to come, baby," he shouts, falling on the edge of the desk as I quickly hold onto his thighs, keeping him in place.

My heart jolts, and my pulse pounds seeing the satisfaction across his face. Popping his balls out of my mouth and standing up, I switch places with him as he catches his breath. I leaned across the desk with my skirt pulled up, panties already off. He smacks and kneads my ass cheeks.

"Where the fuck are your panties, baby?" he questions bending down, kissing the sting away from both cheeks.

"I took them off in the car before I came in. I know how you like easy access."

He scans me critically and beams approval with a head nod. Not waiting, he slides inside my pussy, and I arch my back off the desk from the sudden thrust.

"Fuck!" we both scream at the same time as he spreads my legs even wider for better access. The nearness of his front on top of my back gives me comfort and feelings of protectiveness. His warm hot groans and moans near my ear tell me all I need to know, and the sweet intoxicating musk of his body is a drug I never want to come down from.

"Baby you're so fucking sexy, your mouth, pussy, everything about you. I cannot wait to make you my wife one day."

"Xavier." I feel a tingling in my toes and I know my orgasm is near.

"This pussy will be the death of me," Xavier says.

I listen to the sounds of our skin slapping together and our groans as he pulls me up from the desk, my back to his front with his arm stretched around to keep me in place. He pounds into my pussy as my heartbeat skyrockets. I bite my bottom lip, gripping his hands as the pleasure overwhelms me. I try to keep myself from getting light-headed. I reach up and grab his arm, hoping to ease his thrusts — a mistake on my part.

"Put your hands down and don't touch me until I tell you to. Do you understand?" he commands as he growls and bites me gently on the neck.

The pit of my stomach churns, and that old familiar feeling comes back to the surface, as that familiar tingle rises into a soul-shattering orgasm. Xavier's harsh, uneven breathing makes a shiver rise up my back. Xavier is coming, and his thrusts are getting faster and faster.

"Come with me now, baby. Shit! Take it all." Xavier moans as he falls forward on top of my back, his breathing uneven, to take the weight off he rolled off me. "I cannot move my legs."

"Neither can I," Xavier responds and pulls me close, cuddling into my side and nuzzling his face in between my shoulder and cheek.

"Are you still meeting your dad before our date?"

Feeling an overwhelming need to sleep, I shake my head no and doze blissfully off in his arms.

AN HOUR LATER, I FEEL Xavier whisper in my ear to wake me up, and I begrudgingly open my eyes, looking around, trying to remember what just happened. I'm on the couch in his office with a blanket draped over me. I finally rise and stretch, watching him walk toward the bathroom, he left the door open and I heard the water running.

"What happened?" I question getting up off the couch and walking toward the bathroom to clean up.

CHAPTER

Thirteen

CHELSEY

"YOU FELL ASLEEP AND I didn't want to wake you, so I let you catch an afternoon nap before our dinner tonight," Xavier says caressing, and smacking my butt, pulling me into his hard chest, I giggled feeling something else trying to wake up for another round.

"Ah. Yeah. I need to shower and head home before Emma calls and yells about us being late. I have no clue who is behind this club or what to expect."

Xavier passes me a toothbrush and a hand towel so I can clean up as he steps out of the bathroom. His lips brush against my cheek. Standing on my tiptoes, I kiss along his lips, now his cheek.

"I texted Jordan to tell your dad that you had a migraine and you couldn't make it over and your father said to call him when you wake up." Xavier says from outside of the bathroom as I head for my purse and shoes.

"Work can wait until tomorrow. What are you wearing tonight?" I ask, checking my phone for any messages.

"Probably the black suit you got me the other day. You know I'm more of a jeans and t-shirt kind of guy unless it's a special occasion. I can't let the guys see my woman looking fashionable with a bum on her shoulders."

"Oh, the black Tom Ford with the gold cufflinks I got you would work perfectly. I have a feeling this club is a big deal. Emma said nothing but high profile people attend, and you have to be invited or referred through the owner," I tell him, linking my arm inside of his as we walk out of his office.

"So how did Emma get an invite?" Xavier questions, opening the door leading me to my car parked in front of his gym.

Once he took over and renovated, the business really took off and I know he plans on opening a second gym really soon. I look at what he's accomplished and a sense of pride fills me. My man is a genius at figuring out what his clientele wants out of a gym experience.

"Her friend works with some big wig client in the night-club industry and invited her to this new club that's been open for a few months. You know, I really like the changes you made with the gym, baby. It's coming along nicely." I answered, watching as the other women watched us as we talked and glaring because he was off limits now, he made it very clear that he was off the market when they tried to ask him out.

We both find ourselves possessive, and have some jealous tendencies when the opposite sex comes around, now that we're together as a couple and in the gym working out more closely. I can't call him out when he gets all alpha in certain situations. If a woman tries to step to him in my face and flirt, we'd have a big problem.

He opens the car door and I throw my purse inside. I kiss his lips one more time before putting the key in the ignition.

"Drive safe and I'll see you in a little bit. I need to wrap up a few things here and go home to shower and change before I pick you up." Xavier leans into my car window.

"I will, see you in a few, babe."

———

TWO HOURS LATER, EMMA, Jordan, Xavier and I stand outside a large black building in downtown Memphis. No cars outside, No lights, No signs. I was afraid we had the wrong location until Emma checked her message invite and it said this is the right spot.

"Emma, did they tell you if someone would be at the door to let us inside?" I inquire frustrated with waiting.

"They said once we arrive the doors would open. I guess the driver that picked us up notifies the owner once a client has been dropped off?" Emma says shrugging.

"I think we have the wrong place," I say, right as the doors open and a tall man in a suit wearing an earpiece motions for us to come inside.

"Kind of rude not to speak, don't you think?" I whisper into Xavier's ear.

He walks ahead of me, holding my hand and keeping a close and protective stance, same as Jordan is with Emma. I hear classical music playing and I jerk back, wondering what type of place Emma has gotten us involved with as we continue walking through a dark hallway.

We make it to another back door and he knocks twice before another security guard opens the door and lets us through without checking our ID.

My mouth drops at the display in front of me. Men and women are dressed in elegant gowns, some even wearing masks as music blasts throughout. We move further into the room and I see a crowd gathered in the corner. Being nosy, I pull away from Xavier and step further into the crowd. Two women are pleasing a man, on their knees, butt naked. Not believing what was happening right in front of me, I glance up and see the last person I'd ever expect to see in a place like this.

"Senator Hill?" I whisper to myself.

CHAPTER

Fourteen

SENATOR HILL & CHELSEY

SENATO HILL

"I CAN'T WAIT TO SEE you in what I bought you tonight," Mason groaned over the phone, causing a shiver to run down my spine. I'd received a package at my door hand delivered and wrapped. I wasn't expecting anything at all. With our lives being as busy as they were, we'd made a deal to not keep in touch. The rules are simple. We meet up, we fuck, and then we go our separate ways.

"Mason," I sighed. The sound of his voice alone caused my clit to throb, I ran a hand between my thighs, picturing that it was his lips. I ran a hand over the red lace corset, thong, and red five-inch heels laid on top of a black box, a black engraved invitation next to the pile requesting my presence tonight.

"Am I hearing distress in your voice, Miss Hill?"

"No, you're hearing the sound of a woman that hasn't had pleasure in a while because of work. It seems your voice is doing something to me, and now I'm running a hand over my breast as I talk with you on the phone."

"You know I don't like it when you touch yourself."

"I guess you'll have to remind me tonight as I wear my new lingerie for you."

"Mhmm. Maya, you know the last thing you want to do is defy me," Mason growled through the phone.

I hang up the phone, leaving him anticipating what our night would be like after the last time we met up. We had tried anal play, and bringing in new partners.

He made the standard arrangements for me to be picked up and escorted through the back alley of the club, so no one would notice me. The dark tinted windows of the vehicle was always a must have whenever we made arrangements to meet up. As the newly elected Senator in Tennessee Congress, it would be all over the media about a state Senator seeking pleasure from a sex club. I've never apologized for my lifestyle, since I'm a single woman. But I knew it would hinder me from getting things done correctly for the people that voted me into office. It didn't make the situation any better that the son of the Speaker of the House in Congress was the one that owned the club.

———

Chelsey

PRESENT.

"OMG!" I whisper under my breath, and a hard body runs into the back of me and grasps my waist tight.

"Excuse me, are you new here?"

Before I can answer, I feel a hard tug on my arm and I fall against Xavier's hard chest.

"Don't fucking touch her," he snaps at the man not knowing he tried to keep me from falling and being clumsy. I try to calm Xavier down, but he moves me behind him as he steps to my defense.

"Wait...baby..."

With my hand on his chest, I whispered to him.

"I'm fine, baby." Time to have some fun."

It felt like tonight was only the beginning of what I could imagine would become a favorite destination.

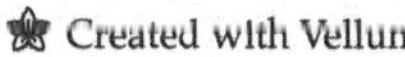

Created with Vellum

Seek To Love

Chelsey

Sometimes in relationships things run their course, but I thought we would never be that couple. I wanted my Happily ever after to continue, but love isn't about the good times, and learning myself everyday in this relationship has brought out a different side of me.

Xavier

She's the one that approached me. I tried to leave her alone, but now we're too deep into things to let anyone come between us. I refuse to let her go and will work to stop anyone, even her own thoughts from causing us to end.

Note: These characters first appeared in (Wet Heat). Seeking in Romance series is dealing with Adult language, explicit content.

NEXT MORNING.

I carried the garbage down the walkway, opened the top, and dropped it inside, before waving over to the neighbor who constantly stuck her nose in anybody's business. Retta was in her late-sixties, widowed, and her kids lived out of the state. Since I moved to the area seven months ago, I'd gotten to know her, and she hung with my mom when she visited. Retta knew everyone's business; even Chelsey's parents came up in conversation sometimes when I was out here doing yard work or working out. I stepped back in the house, shut the screen door, and went to the kitchen to grab a glass of water, kissing the side of Chelsey's neck. She tried to move away, and I shook my head at her little attitude from last night.

"You're not talking to me today."

"Possibly."

"Peanut."

"Xavier."

"Somehow I think this has more to do with your father than me."

She dropped the spatula and turned around, glaring at me.

"My father is not the problem this time."

"What can I do to make it right?"

"We both need to compromise and spend more time together."

"I agree, but you know the second gym is taking up a lot of my time."

"And I'm happy for you but remember what matters."

"I will. So, how are things coming along at the bank?"

Chelsey shrugged and turned back around, picking up the spatula to plate the pancakes, eggs and place them on the table in front of me.

"I'm thinking of leaving the bank."

"You've always loved working there."

"I do, but my father is putting more pressure on me."

"Come work for me."

Her eyes lit up at my suggestion.

"Thank you for the offer, but that would be too much."

"Why do you say that?"

"Xavier, you ignore all the women flirting with you, but I see it, and I'd be ready to fight them."

I chuckled at her statement, and she hated the stories of how women come in the gym and want to get a one-on-one session. She even worked out in some of the class sessions. Some of the women knew she was my girlfriend, but they didn't care.

"Sorry, baby. I'll do better to put a stop to them flirting." I kissed her cheek.

"Thank you. What are your plans for today?" She scooped oatmeal in her mouth.

She wanted to go on a diet, and I often complained because in my eyes, she was perfect the way she was. I didn't care about her being a size zero or twenty. I loved every curve, stretch mark, smooth mound of her breasts, and sweet brown skin. The relationship we had was bumpy in the beginning. Her parents weren't too happy that she was dating a blue-collar type of guy with baggage from his upbringing. Plus, her family was well known in Tennessee, and my family was known as the black sheep. We made it work and became even closer, and things were looking up until recently.

"Meet up with Jordan and Mason at the gym."

"I have to see my mom, then run to the bank for a few minutes."

"Let's plan a date."

"Tonight?"

"Yeah, what do you want to do?"

Chelsey pushed her fork over into my plate and picked up a piece of pancake.

"Can we go to the club?"

"You can have whatever you want."

"What if I wanted to do something different at the club?"

"I don't share."

She snickered and stretched her hand out to palm my wrists.

"I know, but I was thinking we could try some new things out in the bedroom."

"Should have started the conversation off like that."

"Stop being so uptight." She rose, pecked me on the lips, picked her dishes up, and went to the sink.

"I told you long ago, you're mine."

I followed to put the leftover food in the trash and helped wash the dishes before showering and going off to work.

———

An hour later, I was inside my second location, teaching a class, and watched to make sure everyone was doing the steps correctly. I didn't teach as much as I used to in the beginning because the business side of things took up most of my time. I'd planned to have my assistant handle more of the workload, but I had control issues, and leaving anything up in the air would drive me crazy.

"Xavier, can you help me with my back?" LoriAnn called out from the second row. She was one of the ladies Chelsey had talked about flirting with repeatedly. rEver since she got her breast implants, she thought that would be a turn on for me, which was further from the truth. I liked my women natural, intelligent, and a great personality.

"You look to be doing okay to me," I said, standing next to her. I pushed the microphone up and turned the music volume low.

"I think I'm missing the correct pose; can you help me please?" She batted her eyelashes and smiled. I knew what she was doing, but I refused to fall into her trap, especially with Emma being here and staring. Jordan was planning on meeting me here soon, and Emma would run her mouth and say I was doing something I wasn't.

"Spread your legs a little further out. Overall, you got this," I replied, continuing to walk around the room. I checked to make sure everybody was comfortable and getting what they needed out of the session.

"All right, folks. Another great day. I hope you enjoyed it. Make sure to check the schedule for the next session."

"What if we want a private session?" LoriAnn blurted out, tossing her blond hair into a high ponytail.

"I no longer do private sessions, but my team can help you out."

"But I want you." She stepped in front of me and ran her finger down my arm.

"Xavier, have you talked to Chelsey today?"

I smirked, looking up at Emma as she stared at Lori-Ann's hand on my arm.

"Yes, we're planning a date tonight. Why?"

"You have a girlfriend?" LoriAnn asked.

"He does, so I'd advise you to knock off the flirting," Emma informed her. Out of the corner of my eye, I saw Jordan hold his finger up to his lips, creeping up behind Emma.

"Excuse me—"

"LoriAnn!"

Jordan bearhugged her from behind and twirled her in a circle.

"Put me down!" she snapped, clenching her fist and hitting him on the back.

I laughed and stepped around LoriAnn to gather my bag and clean up the equipment from the class. LoriAnn took that as her cue to leave, which I was grateful for. Emma was a spitfire like Chelsey when she was pushed.

"Man, what are you doing, messing with people." Jordan put Emma down on the floor.

"If Chelsey is not here, who else will have her back?" Emma replied.

"Not your job, Emma."

"Jordan, shut up and worry about yourself. I know you've been looking at other women," Emma fussed, took the keys out of his hands, and marched out of the room in a huff.

"Women, man." Jordan picked up one of the rugs off the floor to help me clean up.

"Is she still accusing you of stepping out?" I asked. Emma recently had a baby and worked on losing some of the baby weight, but she still felt like Jordan was cheating, even though they'd been married for a year.

"Same thing, different day. We'll be fine."

"I understand."

"My sister is acting funny."

"I think your father is starting up again."

"He was pissed about you guys living together?" Jordan asked.

"Probably, but it's mostly us not spending time together."

"You have to make it a priority. I'm taking Emma on a little couples trip."

"Where?"

I left the room, marked off the class, and blocked off the rest of my day with the front desk. Jordan went to the bar I had installed for the new location. A few minutes later, Jordan set the peach-lime smoothie on the desk, and I thanked him.

"We're heading to Jamaica for a few days."

"Who's keeping Jr.?"

"My parents."

"You guys deserve a little getaway."

"Being married comes with adjustments, so I'm not knocking Emma for feeling lonely."

My brow hiked at his admission.

"Is there something you need to tell me?"

"Bro, cut it out. I'm not cheating."

I raised my hands in shudder.

"I didn't say you were. Just need to know if I should get a spare room set for you," I joked. His eyes drew into slits.

"Not funny."

"I hear you, but what are you doing tonight?"

"Nothing but hanging with my kid and Emma."

"I'm going to the club with Chelsey."

"Spare me the details please."

"It's your fault we even know about the place."

"You always throw that in my face."

"Fuck you."

"But for real, my sister loves you. Ignore what naysayers throw your way."

"Thanks, bro." We shook hands, and I continued shuffling through orders.

"Have you thought of expanding the business more?"

"I am, and it's one cause of contention in my relationship."

"She thinks you'll have less time for her?"

"I've been on a kick of wanting everything perfect."

"That's understandable as a new businessman."

"Yeah, but I do stay here late at night sometimes, or come in extra early."

"Gotcha."

"Not good."

"Nope, especially if you want to eventually marry."

A knock at the door interrupted us, and I motioned for Mason to come in and take a seat.

"We were just talking about you."

"Whatever it is, leave me out of it please." He slugged his gym bag on the floor.

"Are you just getting in now?" I questioned.

"Yeah, I had an early meeting."

"We need a room reserved."

"Just called my assistant to hold one and tell her I said the top room."

"Thanks."

"No problem. So, how are things?" Mason picked up a piece of candy from the jar on my desk.

"Women."

"When are you planning to marry Chelsey?" he asked.

"More than likely after I have the next location up and running."

He and Jordan looked at each other.

"What?"

"All I'm going to say is that waiting too long can be disaster."

"Thanks, Oprah."

"Chelsey wants to get married," Jordan said.

"I know that, and I want to marry her, but not yet."

"Putting work before your relationship is not a good idea," Mason said.

Everyone knows I grew up poor and struggled to make ends meet once I got into what I loved to do and have the person I loved by my side. Att the same time, she came from wealth and was used to having money and her lifestyle. I planned to make sure it continued once we got married.

"I got this, guys."

CHAPTER

Sixteen

CHELSEY

I LIED and told Xavier I was only visiting with my mother and then some bank work, but I failed to mention I had an appointment with my doctor because I'd felt a little off lately. I was afraid it could be something serious and not knowing would stress me out even more. Dr. Abrams wrote in her notes as I sat up from the table and pulled the gown down.

"All right, Chelsey, so how long have you been feeling off?"

"About a month now."

"Have your periods been regular?" she questioned.

"Yeah, are you saying I'm pregnant?"

"No, I will have to wait and see what the test results are."

"Extra tired from working a lot."

"Are you putting in more hours than usual?"

"Yes."

She dropped the pen, removed her glasses, and sat back in the chair.

"We talked about your workload, Chelsey."

"I know, Dr. Abrams."

"Call me Chloe, but I think it's stress."

"Really think so?"

"Not to worry. Take a vacation or cut your workload down."

"I promise I will."

"Good, I'll call you in a few days with results."

We hugged, and I got dressed and set up an appointment to come back in a few months. I picked up my phone, walked to my car, and dialed Emma's number.

"Hey, lady."

"Hello."

"Where are you? You sound windy."

"Getting in my car, leaving the store."

"Well, I'm sitting here with throw up on my boobs from your nephew."

I laughed, turned out of the parking space, and headed through the green light. I propped my phone on the stand to talk on speaker.

"Leave my baby alone."

"Your baby is messy."

"Awww, Jr. is sweet."

"That's a lie."

"You need a girls' day out. What about lunch and the spa?"

"That sounds great, but your brother has planned a trip for us."

"What! When does this happen?"

"In two weeks, Jamaica."

"That sounds exciting."

"I can't wait to be buck naked on the beach." She laughed, and I chuckled at her statement.

"Have fun for me then."

"Why don't you come with Xavier?"

"He's too busy. Plus, my schedule is mounting."

"Too much work for me."

"Change the subject. How was class earlier?"

"It was fine, besides LoriAnn's ass."

"What she do now?"

"Her usual flirting and trying to suck Xavier's dick through his shorts."

We burst into laughter at her comment. I slowed through a yellow light and made it a block away from my job.

"Girl, LoriAnn is a mess."

"She really is and so desperate."

"Let her keep on with the mess."

"Why does she think she can have my man?"

"I don't know, but you better inform her before I do."

"You're right."

"Let me call you back. This boy is crying up a storm."

"No worries. Give him a kiss for me. I just made it to work."

"Sounds good. Call me on your lunch break."

"Okay. Bye, girl."

I ended the call and shut the door, holding on my brief-case and purse. I spoke to the security guard and staff, then sauntered to my office. I dropped my bags on the floor next to my desk and hit the answering machine for messages.

"Hey, Chelsey. You have an appointment."

"Who is it? I wasn't expecting anyone."

"A Ryan Barnes," she whispered, biting her nail.

"Candice, please be professional."

"Sorry."

"Send him back here." I bent down to open my briefcase and take out the banking loans I needed to approve. I heard someone whistle, and I jumped up fast.

"Sexy."

"Huh?"

"You're sexy."

A lump formed in my throat. The dark-brown eyes

staring back at me looked like a lion ready to pounce on his prey. I would never cheat, but something about this man seemed odd and familiar.

"Ryan Barnes." He stuck his hand out for a shake.

"Chelsey, president of the bank."

"I know. You don't remember, do you?"

"No, have a seat."

He chuckled, opened his jacket, and sat with his legs gaped open. Ryan looked to be as tall as Xavier with all thirty-two teeth. Dimples on both sides of his cheek, light brown skin, low trim fade.

"I worked with your father."

"Oh."

"He told me I should meet with you about my company looking to do investments."

"Well, my father was mistaken, Ryan. We're not doing investments."

"He said you'd say that."

"My father tells a lot of lies."

"I think the last time we saw each other, we had a charity event together."

"That's where I know you from."

"Yeah, a children's charity my company helped sponsor."

"I hope you find the investors, but right now, that's not something I'm interested in doing."

"No problem, thought I'd ask. What about dinner?"

I stood, and he rose out of his seat. I rounded the desk and opened the office door for him to leave.

"I have a boyfriend."

"You're still with that handyman."

"Handyman?"

He nodded.

"Xavier's a businessman with two gyms that are very well known in town and across the country."

"Ouch! Sorry, didn't mean to step on your toes."

"I know what you meant, and you can tell my father it won't work."

"Touché."

He walked out of my office, and I slammed the door behind him and started to work. I lifted the phone to put in a lunch order, and Maya poked her head in my office.

"Am I interrupting?" she asked.

"Hey! I haven't seen you in forever, Senator Hill." I reached out for a hug.

"I know. I thought I'd pop in on my way to work to say hi."

"You look gorgeous."

"So do you. How are things going around here?" She motioned around my office.

My head tilted to the side in thought, and I pursed my lips.

"Exhausting."

"I told the girls that when I'm back in town, we all should get together for a girls trip or something."

"How is everything in politics?"

"Up and down as usual."

"How precious is this little one?"

"She's beautiful, funny, and sweet. How is your family?"

"You know my brother just had a baby boy, and he's married."

"Your parents must be happy."

"They've spoiled him so much."

"Probably waiting on you to have one."

"That won't happen for a while."

"You're not interested in having a family?"

"In the future, but we're living together now, and I like it being just us."

"I get it. Mason and I were just having fun in the beginning. Soon, we just became husband and wife."

"One day I'll get there."

"Well, I won't hold you up. Get back to work." Maya reached over for a hug, and I waved goodbye. I grabbed my cell and dialed my parents at home to talk with my father.

"Hello."

"Hi, Mom."

"Hey, Chelsey."

"Is Dad there?"

"No, he's at some busy meetings."

"What happened to him retiring?" I questioned.

"Your father will never stop working."

"Well, can you relay a message that he needs to stop trying to interfere in my love life."

"What did he do?"

"You remember Ryan Barnes?"

"That name sounds familiar."

"He owns a lot of real estate properties and has a charity we contributed to."

"Oh, right, I remember."

"Yeah, he just showed up here in my office."

"Maybe he wanted to do business."

"Mom, I'm not stupid."

"All right, I'll talk with your father."

"Thanks, please tell him this was the last straw."

"Chelsey."

"I'm serious. Get over it. Xavier is my forever."

THE CLUB WAS CROWDED TONIGHT, and I was happy Xavier reserved a room tonight and ordered us drinks and a light meal. I removed my jewelry and stood naked in front of him as he held onto anal beads in his hand.

"Turn around," he commanded, and I nodded, doing as he instructed and climbing on top of the bed. I felt his warm hands caress my ass. I watched him pick up the bottle of lube and pop it open to prepare for what was to come.

"Take a deep breath, baby," he said. I felt an intense pressure once he pushed each bead in slowly. Clenching my teeth, I squeezed the sheets in my hand as he came up behind me and pushed my legs close together as I lay flat on my stomach. Tonight, he'd wanted to be gentle and take his time exploring my body and giving into my desires. Feeling his kisses down my back to each ass cheek, he separated and pushed his large girth in my pussy. A lump formed in my throat, knowing how good he made me come at times. Sometimes, it became a game to see if I'd squirt on command.

"Fuck me… Yes, right there," I panted, trying to push back into him. Often, he'd tell me to bring him to his knees, but he couldn't imagine what it felt like to have him moaning and rumbling under his breath.

"Shit…" He buried his nose in the pillow next to me, grinding back and forth.

"Harder, X," I cried out, needing him to lose control.

"You feel that?" he questioned, giving me punishing deep thrusts. Our skin smacked against each other until he abruptly pulled out and turned me over. He lifted me around the waist halfway, bent his legs, and slid back in to pump faster. I propped myself up with my hands, barely able to control the orgasm that lingered in my core. Something about these new tricks turned me on even more.

"Mmmm… Ohhh God… .Xavier," I screamed when he lifted me up and stepped off the bed, still holding me around the waist. I reached out to grab the back of his head and smashed my mouth on his. The tingling feeling rose, and Xavier pushed my left leg down and propped my right leg up in his arm. He thrusted from the bottom, and I felt my soul leave my body at him slamming into me hard.

"The room is spinning… Ahh!"

"Your pussy is choking my dick."

"Please can I come?" I asked.

"Damn, come now," he grunted, moved his hand, and rubbed my clit.

"Ughh… Xavier." My head fell onto his shoulder.

His tongue snaked his way through my lips. I rubbed the back of his head.

"I love it when you get flexible," he whispered in my ear.

———

Three days later.

Tonight, we had family dinner with my parents and my brother, his wife Emma. Xavier was dressed nicely, and I threw on a simple black, knee-length dress with wide straps. Xavier held my hand. and I knocked, leaning my head on his shoulder.

"Hopefully we don't stay long."

"Let's pray everybody is cool tonight." Xavier responded, knocking on the door again. The butler opened it and smiled.

"Miss Chelsey," Anderson said.

"Hi, Anderson."

I removed my coat, and he took it, hanging up, along with Xavier's. We headed into the family room and heard laughter. I smiled at my nephew in my brother's arms and glanced around the room full of guests. My mouth dropped open in shock.

"There's Chelsey," Gerald blurted out. All eyes looked at us.

Ryan was here with an older couple I assumed were his parents. He looked gorgeous with a fresh, trimmed beard. He wore a black Tom Ford suit, which I guessed from a glance because I had purchased the same thing for Xavier months back. I grew heated in annoyance that my father would stoop so low after everything we'd been through to become a family again. He promised to make an effort with me being in a relationship with Xavier, but that was all a lie from the simple fact Ryan showed up at my office. Now, he was here at their house.

"Peanut, you good."

I cleared my throat.

"Yes, I'm fine. Why do you ask?"

"You went blank for a second."

"Finally, Princess has arrived," Jordan joked, walked over to Xavier, and dapped, then gave me a hug.

"Shut up, Jordan." I pushed him in the shoulder.

"Not my fault you take forever to get dressed," Jordan complained. I rolled my eyes and grabbed my nephew.

"Come here, Auntie's baby."

Emma passed him over, and I kissed his chunky cheeks. I was planning to ignore everyone except Jordan and Emma. You would never catch me disrespecting my parents, but I was good with ignoring them to keep the peace and from keeping Xavier out of the games my father was playing. I walked down the hall to the kitchen to grab a bottle for Jr. and a drink for me.

"Are you planning to ignore me all night?"

My back stiffened. I felt my skin get warm, as my nephew continued sucking on his bottle without a care in the world. I turned around to face the culprit and put on a fake smile so the chef wouldn't freak out.

"Mr. Barnes, it's nice to see you again."

I pulled the bottle from my Jr.'s mouth and held him on my shoulder to pat his back.

"Is that your boyfriend?"

"Mr. Barnes, how is that any of your business?"

"You're cute when you're upset."

"I know. My man tells me that all the time."

He smirked and slid his tongue over his top lip.

"Chelsey, you good?" Xavier approached, stood to the side of me, and stared at Ryan.

"Ryan, and you are?" He reached a hand out toward Xavier.

"Someone you don't want to know about."

Eighteen

XAVIER

THE GUY LOOKED from me toward Chelsey, like they held a secret that shouldn't get out, but I knew all her old boyfriends. If you want to call them boyfriends; we ran every guy away who tried to talk to her.

"No offense, but Chelsey was introducing me to her nephew."

"You see him. Anything else?"

"What's your name again?"

"I didn't give it."

Chelsey held her hand out, blocking me from charging at him.

"Ryan, I think you better go," she said.

The cockiness on his face went away. He seemed more nervous when my fists drew at my side. I tdidn't play about a lot of things, and Chelsey was one of them. I caught on as soon as we walked in that her parents were trying to set her up with him. All this time of him pretending to be cool with me was fake and phony. For Chelsey's sake, I never said a word, but tonight went overboard.

"You okay." She wrapped her arm around my waist and

leaned into my chest. I took Jr. out of her hold and held him in my arms.

"I'm fine, but your little boyfriend's going to get his ass kicked."

She slapped me on the chest.

"He's not my boyfriend."

"You sure, because he's really working on trying to be."

"I already have a boyfriend."

"What's his name?"

"Xavier."

"Good girl." I bent down, ran my tongue across her lips, pushed my tongue through, and sucked on her bottom lip.

"Eww… don't do that nasty shit in front of my son," Jordan barked, grabbing his son out of my hands.

"Shut up, Jordan. You act like you don't do worse in front of him." Chelsey pinched his arm. He stepped out of her way, as she chased him around the island in the kitchen.

"Jr., you see your auntie. Nasty, man," Jordan joked, and I chuckled and held my hand up to cover my laugh.

Chelsey's face grew into a grimace.

"Stop telling him that stuff. Babies retain the stupid shit you say."

"Chelsey, are you going to ignore your parents all night?" Jordan stopped running, passed his son back to Chelsey, and grabbed a bottle of water out of the fridge.

"Yep, so don't get on my bad side, or join my list." Chelsey strolled out of the kitchen, we followed as she played with the baby.

The dining room table was set for a large party, but it was a small gathering, so this told me her parents wanted to impress him and his parents.

"Xavier, I'm glad you could come, but Chelsey said your businesses have taken off?" Lynidas asked.

I pulled the chair out for Chelsey and sat next to her. Ryan sat across next to his parents.

"Chelsey wanted me here, so I make sure to spend as much time together as we can."

"He's even thinking of opening a third fitness center," Chelsey replied.

"Does that really bring in any money?" Gerald asked.

"Daddy, we talked about this."

"Tonight is about family, and new business. Mr. Barnes is looking to expand his business." Lynidas held her glass up for toast.

"I went by Chelsey's office earlier today, but she declined my offer," Ryan said.

I clenched the napkin in my hand, as he stared at Chelsey and smirked. Swiftly I glanced at her to meet her eyes, and she quickly handed Jr. to Emma.

"Xavier, let's go." Chelsey jumped up out of her seat.

"We haven't had dinner yet, Chelsey," Lynidas said.

"I lost my appetite," Chelsey replied and walked out of the dining room.

"Ryan, I apologize for my daughter's behavior. I will get you with the right people," Gerald answered.

I saved and worked to get everything I had now and to be with Chelsey I knew she was a prize. She was expected to date a guy on a certain financial level to provide for her. For him to stand in my face after we talked and made some type of resolution. Chelsey had no problems out of our relationship.

"Let's go."

"I'll call you tomorrow, Peanut," Jordan said. She kissed her nephew on the lips, and I grasped her hand and walked out together, not looking back.

———

The following day, I had Morris and Warren follow up on Ryan Barnes and his business. Their work not only involved securing events but delved into background checks and private investigation if needed. I knocked on the door of Morris' office and waited to be let inside.

"It's open!" he called out.

I turned the knob and walked in to see Lisa sitting on the edge of his desk.

"Hey, Xavier!" Lisa said.

"How are you, Lisa?"

We hugged, and I sat in the chair across from his desk.

"I'm doing good. Actually, I'm meeting Chelsey later for shopping and lunch."

y"Try not to spend too much of my money," Morris blurted out. She rolled her eyes, pecked him on the lips, and grabbed her purse to leave. Morris opened the desk drawer, pulled a yellow envelope, and tossed it on top of the desk in front of me.

"What did you find?"

I flipped it over and took out stacks of photos and documents with Ryan's name on the label.

"He's looking to make a name for himself, working with a lot of big-time people."

"Looks like he's skimmed some money off the top."

"He's good, but most importantly, Chelsey was right to not work with him."

"Did you tell her?"

He shook his head.

"No, I thought it should come from you."

"Yeah, her father is adamant about doing business with him." I looked at the numbers and noticed a lot of money changing hands.

"You'll see even more photos of Chelsey there at the club and work."

My nose flared looking over the photos he had taken of my girl and me together. This was a game to him, and I wasn't one to play games when it came to my woman.

"What do you want to do?"

Irritation at him grew, and my pulse raced.

"I'll handle him."

I stood, and Morris jumped up and held his hand out to block me from leaving.

"I didn't give you that information to possibly end up in jail."

"Don't worry. I'll have a little conversation with him and be on my way."

Morris chucked his chin up.

"Just a conversation."

"I'm a businessman first."

"Yeah, but we both know how you are about Chelsey."

I growled at his comment, bringing up the past when Mason mistook her for someone else, and we almost got into a fight.

"Sounds like you're worried about me."

"Any friend of Lisa's, I have to protect. Chelsey is her friend, which means we look out for each other."

"Thanks, Morris, but I promise not to kill him. A black eye, now that's different."

I smacked the papers against my hand and marched out of his office to find Mr. Barnes and catch up on some things.

THE MALL WAS CROWDED, and I held two bags in my hands from Lane Bryant. I needed some more comfortable clothing before the winter time got here and some rain boots I'd been eyeing for the longest time. My father tried calling me earlier today, and I ignored his call and met up with the girls for a day of pampering before Emma went on her trip.

"Let's go in here." Emma pointed at Victoria's Secret. We followed, and I saw a black silk robe with a matching bra set. I picked it up to check the price and look for my size.

"You ready for your trip, Emma?" Lisa asked.

"Yes, I can't wait to be on a beach with my boo." Emma picked through the row of red stockings and bras.

"How long are you guys going for?"

"A week," Emma replied, holding a bra up to show us.

"That's cute. Try a pink or lavender color," I suggested, going to the rack of tights and pajama pants.

"Why didn't we get invited?" Lisa wondered.

"For real, I'm done filming for two months. I need a vacation," Kyla pouted, holding three pairs of socks and thongs.

"This is a reconnection trip for me and Jordan," Emma answered, and I nodded in agreement. She'd been working nonstop as a stay-at-home mom. Plus, with Jordan working nonstop, they needed time together as much as me and Xavier.

"Well, we can plan something for couples next time."

"I vote for that." Maya joined us, and we all screamed and crowded around her as security stood, blocking people off. I should have asked to have the store closed for us to shop privately since we had a politician and actress, along with Lisa in attendance.

"Maybe we should get out of here. The place is getting a lot of attention," Emma suggested.

"Are you done shopping?" I questioned.

"Just need these." She held up a thong set, switched over to the register, and I laughed.

"You won't even have that on long enough once Jordan sees you wearing them."

"That's true. Our love life has been in a little rut," Emma complained.

"Preaching to the choir." I raised my hand.

"Strong women with hot guys, and no time to fuck. What is the world coming to now?" Lisa joked, and I chortled and placed money down to pay on my nightgown set.

"I could go for something to eat."

"Where do we want to go?" Lisa asked.

"Try that pizza place on Third and Poplar Avenue," Kyla said.

"No, I'm tired of crowds. Let's go to my place and order food," I said.

All the girls agreed and finished paying for their items. Lisa and Kyla piled into my car, and Maya told the security team to follow her in mine since Emma drove her car, and she would ride with her.

———

Thirty minutes later, we sat out by the pool in the back with bottles of wine, fruit, cheese tray, with a variety of meals from salads, fish tacos, and pizza. I opened a bottle of wine and served the drinks, while Maya fixed the plates as they lounged near the cabana deck.

"So, Morris wants me to move to Vegas," Lisa blurted out, taking a gulp of her wine.

All of them gasped in response, and I sipped my drink.

"What do you want?" Maya asked.

"I might feel the same way." Lisa shrugged her shoulders.

"Warren and I are splitting time between Vegas and here. He's also expanding into Chicago," Kyla told me.

"I feel like Xavier and I are drifting apart."

"Wait! Why am I the last to know all this?" Maya argued.

"You're a senator, wife, and mother, Maya."

"We can't come to you with all our problems." Lisa walked up to the table and poured more wine.

"I understand, but I feel like our little group is growing apart. I just met Emma." Maya pointed toward Emma and bit into her pizza.

"We have to make a promise to stay in touch."

"No matter what, we'll always have our group chats." Lisa laughed and shimmied in her seat.

"This is like a full-circle moment."

"What do you mean?" Emma said.

"Because of you, we went to Club Seek, and they found men." I pointed at Emma.

"Ohhh, that's right. That's for helping me find the best pussy eater in the world." Lisa snapped her finger and held her glass up in the air. Everyone burst into laughter as Emma spat out her drink.

"Lisa, some things you can keep to yourself," Maya fussed.

"I know, Maya, but don't act like Mason doesn't have your toes circling," Lisa replied.

"I've been feeling a little off lately," I said, quickly draining my glass of alcohol. I reached for another bottle, and Lisa slapped my hand away.

"What do you mean off?"

"Tired, not able to eat. I went to the doctor."

"When did this happen?"

"A few days ago."

"When were you going to tell us?"

"Dr. Abrams is running tests."

"Call her." Lisa dug into her purse and pulled her cell phone out.

"Her office is probably closed. It's going on four in the afternoon." I looked down at my watch.

"We're best friends, almost sisters. Hell, she's your sister-in-law, and you kept this from her," Lisa argued.

"Maybe you're pregnant," Kyla blurted, grabbed some tacos off the table.

"I'm not ready for that."

"You're never ready," Maya and Emma said at the same time.

"What did Xavier say?" Lisa questioned.

"He doesn't know."

"Chelsey," Emma fussed.

"Our schedules are crazy right now, then there was the mess with my father at the house."

"What happened to that?" Lisa questioned.

Emma and I peered at each other.

"My dad tried to set me up."

"With another guy? Like a date?" Lisa asked.

"More like a marriage," Emma muttered.

"Had the guy come to my job, then my parents' house with his parents," I said.

"Wow," Maya said.

"I refuse to call them."

"Even your mom." Kyla passed Emma some of her food and sat at the edge of the chair.

"I'll call her in a few days, but it's mostly my dad."

"You're doing the right thing. Ignore him," Lisa said.

"Xavier was ready to kick his ass at the table." I chuckled.

"That plays no games about you," Kyla said.

"I know."

CHAPTER

Twenty

XAVIER

I PUSHED *him up against the wall, held my arm up against his neck, and placed pressure with my fists balled up.*

My thoughts went from talking to wanting to punch, then shoot him in my mind. I didn't need to be away from Chelsey, so I optioned for talking unless he got out of hand.e

"Mr. Barnes, Xavier is here to see you."

"Send him in, Rachel."

She waved me in, and I smiled politely and watched her close the door. I locked it and held the envelope in my hand. He stood, buttoning his jacket behind his desk.

"Xavier, what do I owe for this visit?" Ryan picked up the envelope I had tossed on his desk.

"You've been stalking my girl."

He chuckled.

"I don't need to stalk."

"Oh, because you have money, right?"

"Money, charm, world class."

"Look, you piece of shit!"

"I can have security here in a split second."

"Fuck your security."

"It's not my fault her parents want her with me."

"Chelsey doesn't want you."

"Did she say that?"

"I'm going to say this for the last time, because I know she already spoke to you. Leave Chelsey alone."

"Or what?"

"Find out."

"If we do business together, maybe I'll back off."

I chortled at his comment.

"The business you're stealing from me, right?"

"You can't prove that."

"Try me and see. If you come in contact with Chelsey or her father."

He blew out a breath and waved me off. I started to charge toward him.

"Okay, I'll stay away." He held his arms up in surrender.

"That's a safe bet."

I double checked the collar around her neck and peered in her eyes as she watched my every move. Tonight, we decided to take it another step further with her chained by a spreader bar separating her legs and hands in suspension in the air. Her curvy full figure was a beautiful sight to see, and I decided to turn the video on. I needed a reminder of this for when we were alone again and needed inspiration. Chelsey moaned as my hand ran down from her ankle to her inner thigh. I smelled her sweet arousal, and my dick hardened and jumped, ready to dig into her walls.

"She's already screaming for me."

Chelsey nodded and gasped when I slid not one, but two fingers inside.

"Taste yourself, baby." I lifted my finger to her lips.

"Mmmm…"

"You're about to be fucked so hard."

"Please."

"You're my queen, remember that."

"You're my king."

I couldn't wait any longer and pushed forward to her asshole. I felt her tense up and lovingly tweaked her nipples, kissed her lips, and teased her clit to loosen her up.

"Just a little more, baby."

"Oh… Yes." She gasped.

"Oh, fuck!" I moaned and felt her rock back and forth, meeting my thrusts.

"Xavier!"

"I need you to come on my tongue." I suddenly pulled out, dropped to my knees, sucking, slurping, and twirling my tongue on her wet, gushy sex. Hearing her screams and shouts of pleasure gave me motivation to never lose sight of what I had in front of me. My past could never compare to what my future looked like before me.

"Shittt…" she moaned and squirted in my mouth, and I stood back up, shoved my dick in her tight pussy, and muttered more curse words under my breath once I came behind her. I bent over, deepened our kiss, and sucked on her tongue. Seeing the exhaustion on her face, I stood and reached for the towel from the back of the chair, wiped us off, and unhook the chains.

"You ready for bed?"

"I'm ready to go home."

"As you wish…"

I kissed the top of her forehead and helped her down, and we redressed and left for home.

———

The next day, I drove with Chelsey to her doctor's follow-up appointment to get her results. I was more nervous than she was, and I couldn't fathom her being sick and not waking up to her face every day.

"Stop worrying." I held her hand up, kissing her palm.

"Trying to stay positive, but what if..."

"No what ifs. We don't think like that."

"Thank you for coming with me."

"Never worry about me being at your side."

"So, something interesting happened early today when you were in the shower," Chelsey said.

"What?"

"My father called and apologized."

"Your father?" I turned at the light into the parking structure, went to a spot near the door, and cut the car off.

"Yes, I know."

"What did he say?"

"He loves me and said Ryan's not going to bother me again."

"I'm happy to hear that, baby."

"Xavier."

"Yeah?" I opened the passenger door to help her out.

"Did you do something to Ryan?"

"Chelsey, you know me, baby."

"That's the point."

"Stop worrying about somebody that isn't in her world view." I lifted her chin, pressed a kiss on her lips, and smacked her on the ass. Holding the door open, she swished in front of me, making me adjust myself.

"Hi Chelsey, the doctor is ready for you."

"Great, thank you."

"Follow me back." The office assistant pushed the door open and let us in to have a seat to wait.

"Are you nervous?" Chelsey questioned.

I reached over and grasped both her hands. She looked into my eyes.

"No reason to be nervous. We're good, and you'll be

fine." I bent down, slid my tongue over her upper lip, and wrapped her hands around me.

With a knock at the door, the doctor stepped in and cleared her throat.

"Dr. Abrams." Chelsey giggled and wiped her lipstick off my lips.

"Xavier, good to see you again," she said.

"You too, Doc."

"Tell me the truth," Chelsey asked.

"I ran every test, and you're fine. You need to relax and take a vacation," the doctor replied.

"Seriously?" Chelsey said.

"No issues at all?"

"None. She's just stressed and needs to calm down. Her blood pressure is a little high," the doctor answered, pulling out her records.

"Thank you, Doctor."

"No problem. I like you, Chelsey, and want you to stay focused," the doctor said.

"I promise… self-care going forward," Chelsey promised.

Twenty-One

CHELSEY

A MONTH LATER.

I groaned, slamming the alarm off, and rolled over to feel Xavier's side of the bed was empty. I opened one eye and looked around the room. Then Xavier, wearing a pair of boxer briefs, sauntered back into the bedroom from the fog coming from the bathroom.

"Get up, sleepyhead."

"Why! This is supposed to be a vacation," I whined, falling back under the covers.

"As soon as you get up, we can have one." Xavier climbed on the bed and tickled me under the cover.

"Stop!" I screamed, trying to crawl away from him.

"Not until you get up."

"Fine, I'm up."

"Great, per doctor's orders, I want you to relax." Xavier jumped out of bed and extended a hand for me to take.

"What's the plan for today?"

"You shower, have breakfast, and then we head to the beach."

"It's gorgeous here."

"Jordan was able to get a great discount on a last-minute

flight for us, so I wanted to fly you out and enjoy this weekend together."

"You didn't have to do that." I turned the shower on and stripped out of the pajamas I had picked up at Victoria's secret.

"I know, but I wanted to enjoy it all to myself."

"Well, Jamaica is the place to be."

"Might end up wanting to buy a place out here."

"Couldn't hurt to look around." I closed the shower door, grabbing the resort body wash and towel.

"Maybe not today, but we will."

"How about you come and join me?" I pushed the door back open for him to get a glimpse of me in soap suds.

"As tempting as you look, I need to get dressed and make sure breakfast is ready."

"Ugh… you're no fun," I shouted from the other side of the door.

"Later. I'll make it up to you."

———

Two hours after getting dressed and eating breakfast, we went out to the local shops and walked around, meeting new people and sightseeing. I wanted to go to the beach later, once the sun set, and possibly get a quickie in before we went to bed. Xavier didnt't mind, but the shopping part annoyed him because of the amount of stuff I bought. We had to grab a car service to send it all back to the resort and come back to do a second round of shopping.

"This drink is amazing, babe."

"Don't drink too much. I need you ready and aware for tonight."

"Oh, I'll be ready."

"Listen, have you spoken to your father before we came on the trip?"

"Why do you have to spoil the day?"

"I'm not trying to spoil our day."

"Then leave my father out of the conversation."

"Chelsey, at some point you'll need to speak with him."

"I'll talk to my mom."

"Great, but don't isolate your father out."

"Why not?"

"One day, you may need him."

"I have my brother."

"Glad to hear, but a girl needs her father."

He was right. I stayed in touch with my mom cover the past few weeks after the dinner incident. Jordan said he argued back and forth with my dad on my behalf, and I thanked him for stepping in because that man always thought he was right.

I put the drink down on the table, stared out to the ocean, and decided to be spontaneous for once and run out to the beach and let loose.

"Chelsey! Chelsey!" Xavier shouted, ran behind me, and picked me up.

"Ahhh!"

"Woman, what are you doing?"

"I want to get in the water. Put me down."

"Don't scare me like that."

He put me on the ground. I looked to my left, then right, and smirked. I wiggled my brows, lifted my dress, and tossed it on the ground.

"Come catch me," I purred and ran off toward the ocean.

I splashed in, feeling the cool waters. Xavier's eyes darkened,, and I knew the beat was coming out. He'd make me pay for this little rendezvous.

"You're going to pay for that."

"You have to catch me first."

I swam out a little farther, away from any crowds, and

he caught up to me, wrapped his arms around my waist, and pulled me into a kiss.

"Mmmmm...." he moaned, sucked on my lips, and gripped my breasts.

I threw my head back as he peppered kisses along my neck and shoulder. I locked my legs around his waist and felt him push in, stroking me slowly.

"Ughh... Xavier," I panted, tightening my grip to help balance my weight.

"Shit... We need to take this inside."

"Okay... Ahh."

Xavier pulled out of me, swam back to the beach, and led me back to the resort. We went to the shower and ended up back in bed, finishing what I started earlier. Later that evening, after going three rounds, I set up a nice dinner with all his favorites and placed everything on the deck. We sat under the stars and moon, eating and talking.

"You ever think about getting married and having kids?"

"Where did that come from?"

I cut into my calamari and took a piece.

"We never talked about the future."

"You're my future. Wherever you are, I'm there."

"I get that, but you have a booming business. It takes you away."

"Our business."

"Xavier."

"Chelsey, you know my past. It's not pretty."

"Let's drop it."

CHAPTER

Twenty~Two

XAVIER

I'D BEEN HOLDING onto the news that my fitness center would be opening another location and the guys investing to expand it even further. They thought it would be great to open a division in New York, and I was planning to scout some locations. Telling Chelsey now would only start an argument, after bringing up the topic of kids.

"Listen."

"No, I don't want to fight. This is about us enjoying ourselves."

"We are, but I hate to see you pout, so we can shelve this conversation."

"Sure."

"What do you want to do tomorrow?"

"Maybe go scuba diving."

"We can try that."

"Something that gets us really engulfed in the scenery."

"Whatever you want, sweetheart."

"Are you full?"

"I'm stuffed. This was good," I said.

"It's getting late. You want to watch a movie?"

"Yeah, it'll probably put me to sleep."

We grabbed the bottle of wine and stepped in the living room tod set up a movie. She grabbed a blanket out of the bedroom, and I poured us another glass of wine and placed her feet in my lap.

"I could get used to this."

"What, being spoiled?"

"You love spoiling me." She poked her lips out for a kiss, I leaned over, pecked her lips, then rubbed a hand up and down her thigh.

"I do."

"Good."

Two hours later, we were startled out of a sound sleep at the ringing of a cell phone. I looked around and noticed it was her phone ringing.

"Babe, your phone is ringing." I nudged her in the shoulder.

"Huh."

"Your brother is calling."

"Oh… hello," she answered groggily.

She sat up quickly, with a perplexed expression.

"Is he all right!" she shouted.

"What's wrong?"

"Okay, we're leaving now." She hung up the phone and jumped off the couch.

"Chelsey, what's going on."

"We have to go back home; Dad is in the hospital."

I stopped her from pacing and pulled her in my arms to help calm her down. She started to hyperventilate.

"He's going to be fine; I need you to breathe for me, baby."

"Xavier, I can't lose my dad."

"You won't, I promise."

"We need to get a flight out."

"Just pack your things, and I'll handle everything else." I kissed her on the forehead, grabbed our phones, and made some calls to get us back to town fast.

———

I stood off to the side as Chelsey laid her head on her father's chest, while the monitors beeped. The look of relief on her face and his when we made it through those doors must have helped his recovery. He had a mild heart attack and needed to relax, cut out any stress for a while. Jordan stayed up here until we arrived and then went home to be with Emma and his son. Her mom was sleeping in the corner. Chelsey continued talking with her father, and some type of resolution was had because smiles crossed her face and his. Probably knocking on death's door helped him to see that he needed to change his ways and rethink trying to control his kids' lives.

"We'll be up here tomorrow, Daddy," Chelsey said and kissed him on the cheek. He nodded, letting her hand go.

"Xavier," he said.

"Yes, sir." I kicked my foot off the wall, treading toward the end of the bed.

"I'm sorry for everything."

"Me too."

"You're like a son to me, and I treated you horrible."

"No stress, Daddy," Chelsey said.

"Stop smothering me, Chelsey."

He waved her off, and Chelsey rolled her eyes.

He's for sure back to normal," Chelsey muttered.

I chuckled and clasped her hand, leading her out of the hospital room to head home for the night. The next morning, Jordan called to drop off Jr. with Chelsey to keep him while he and Emma helped their mom bring their father home. Standing in the kitchen, I poured coffee and set the table for breakfast, watching her stroll with him in her arms.

"He looks like your brother more and more."

I motioned for her to sit down.

"I know, it's scary."

"How's your dad doing?"

"Better. He has to change his diet and cut out stress."

"Something you know well about."

"I'm going to spend more time with you and my nephew." She lifted him in her arms, and he giggled.

"You look good with a baby in your arms."

She smirked and passed him over to me.

"He's a big boy." Chelsey kissed me on the lips, took her seat again, and poured syrup on her waffles.

"I'm still processing my brother having a kid and Dad almost dying."

"It's going to take time."

"Glad to spend that time with you."

"We already went for two rounds before he got here. Control yourself, Peanut."

"Ughh, I hate when you call me that." She rolled her eyes.

"I know." I chuckled.

"Not the same little kid who had a crush on you when I was younger."

I placed the bottle in Jr.'s mouth and watched him stare into my eyes. I smiled at the innocence across his face.

"You mean the same one who approached me and said they wanted to F.U.C.K."

Her head fell back in laughter.

"He's a baby; he doesn't understand a word you said."

"Doesn't matter. I want to do what my parents didn't do."

"Which is?"
"Protected."
"You're going to be a great dad one day."
"Long as I have you."

Epilogue: Chelsey

One year later.

I closed my eyes and pictured myself on a beach with all my family and friends, laughing and dancing together. The relationship I built with Xavier was a long time coming, and we weathered the storm.

"Chelsey! Push one more time," the doctor demanded. The sweat on my forehead and brow dripped down my nose and cheeks. I did the breathing exercises to keep steady and pushed one more time. I felt a lightness in my body when I heard the cries of my son.

"Chelsey, he's beautiful," Mom said.

I was in a daze and barely could keep my eyes open from the ten hours of labor to get our child here safely. Xavier held him in his arms and walked back over to me, placing him on my bare chest to do skin to skin.

"He looks just like you," I cooed and rubbed the back of his head. Xavier bent down and kissed me on the lips.

"Thank you, Peanut."

"Thank you for being an amazing friend, lover, and husband."

"I can't believe I wasted so long to make you mine."

"It was meant to be like this."

"You're right. Get some rest though; I'll stay up with him."

"What do you want to name him?"

"Michael Xavier."

"He's perfect like his mommy."

He yawned and opened his eyes briefly, and I teared up again, seeing the same ocean-blue eyes like his father. My son would be a heartbreaker, and I needed to prepare myself to not hold on too tight.

"He's starting to cry; I think he's hungry."

"I'll feed him, then you can rock him to sleep," I told Xavier, who helped me pull the gown down and get Michael to latch on properly to right breast. It hurt a little, but I knew this was what I wanted in the beginning when the doctor said I was too stressed and needed to relax. I took her advice and cut my hours at work and spent more time with Xavier, going on trips together. One of those trips ended up being the night we conceived Michael. Now I had all the blessings and the man of my dreams, who I had loved since I could remember.

————

Two years later.

"Do you Xavier take Chelsey to be your husband, in sickness and in health?"

When I thought of my life after giving birth to my son, I never took that day for granted, even when I married Xavier. Here we were years later, and I stopped working at the bank. He opened up a chain of fitness centers, and I was a stay-at-home mom with Michael our little Angel. Xavier wanted more kids, we talked about waiting until Michael is older, in school. After we had our first, I couldn't deny seeing the joy from my family growing.

"I do." Xavier smiled and held onto my hands. We stood in the backyard of our home he had built. Xavier became a multi-millionaire, and no one would ever know. We lived just as modest as we did before.

"Do you, Chelsey—"

"I do!" I yelled excitedly, and our friends and family laughed. The yard was decorated in white and pink with rose petals on the ground. A large sign with our names and the kids hung over the balcony.

"I now pronounce you husband and wife."

Xavier didn't even wait for him to finish, smashing his lips onto my mouth and palming my butt. I extended my arms around his neck. Xavier surprised me with renewing our vows, and I had a surprise for him later when we went to our own private club in the basement.

———

I hope you enjoyed Xavier and Chelsey's story. Also check out more steamy romance with the entire Seek to romance series that includes bodyguard tropes, one night stands, marriage troubles and more here *"Seeking In Romance 1-6"* https://books2read.com/u/4ELGLe

Don't forget if you love Fling romances, bodyguard, forced proximity then check out, **"Protecting Chanel"** https://books2read.com/u/mqwPB8

If you love brother's best friend romance, then you'll love **"Sensual" here** https://books2read.com/u/49lYYM with a dash of steamy romance.

Check out Bodyguard Romance, military, romantic suspense here *"Protecting Bria"* https://books2read.-com/u/bQJkjd

Follow college romance and more characters in *"Taste"* here https://books2read.com/u/bpz1Ng

How about a steamy, medical romance? Check out

"Haven" https://books2read.com/u/4jAvyZ a steamy enemies to lovers romance.

Have you checked out **"His Peace Her Pleasure"**? Click here https://books2read.com/u/3JJr0P a billionaire, steamy romance.

Please also check out my *"Love Don't Live here Anymore Vanessa Andrew"* https://books2read.com/u/mBOWGZ a steamy curvy girl, enemies to lovers romance.

Follow that up with a workplace, vacation romance in **"Love Don't Live Here Anymore Isabella Andrew"** https://books2read.com/u/brVNO7

More workplace, boss romances with **"Love by Design Boxset 1-3"** https://books2read.com/u/m2ldEk

Our relationship started here, so I wanted to celebrate at the place we frequented together and spark up what made us take the step to be together. The kids were home with her parents for the day, so I blocked off the day to spend time with her on our anniversary. She wore a sexy crossbody Ivy Park workout fit. All her curves and fat ass poked out that I loved to taste at night when we were alone.

"Xavier!" she gasped when my hand went to her lower back and peeled back the shorts. She kicked them off, showing only a red thong. I smacked her ass, watched it jiggle, and kissed each cheek.

"I want you to do five pushups."

"What do I get in return?" she questioned.

"I want you face down, ass up with me over you as you rise."

"Somehow I think this won't be an actual workout."

"It can be."

The smirk I held showed I was planning something else behind my little suggestion. I had the whole place locked down for the day and put on some music, brought drinks and food in case we needed them. She turned around, got in position, and started to drop to the floor, I pushed her legs together in the proper form. Then I removed my shirt and shorts.

"What are you doing?" She licked her lips.

"We're going to start with me behind you as you come up.:

"Your dick is going to be poking me."

"That's the point, my love."

"Somehow I knew you'd make these torturous."

"If you do a full push up, I'll give you a reward either with my tongue or my dick."

"If I can't?"

"You don't get either."

"That's not fair."

"I promise, by the end of this workout, you won't be sweaty from just pushups."

She rolled her eyes, turned around back into her normal form, and lifted, causing her ass to graze the tip of my dick.

"Oh, God."

"It's only me here, baby."

Spotify PlayList

1. BEYONCE: DEJAVU
2. Chaka Khan: Ain't Nobody
3. Jill Scott: Crown Royal
4. Anita Baker: I Apologize
5. Luther Vandross: A House is Not A Home
6. Monica: Commitment
7. Normani: Waves
8. Pink Please Don't Leave Me.
9. No Doubt: Don't Speak
10. Rihanna: You Da One
11. D'Angelo: Lady
12. Rihanna: Hard

About the Author

A TENNESSEE NATIVE, and California dreaming Author KeKe Renée is living and striving to continue her passion of writing short story romances in genres ranging from Erotic, Paranormal, and Women's Fiction.

Catalogue of Releases By Keke Renée:

- Wet Heat (Wet Heat Series Book 1)
- Every time We Touch Novelette (Wet Heat Book 2 Series)
- His Peace, Her Pleasure
- Baby, It's Cold Outside
- Love Don't Live Here Anymore, Vanessa Andrew Book 1
- Love Don't Live Here Anymore, Isabella Andrew Book 2
- One Night Only-A Novelette (Love By Design Book 1)
- Cassian and Savannah (Love By Design Book 2)
- Deidra's Love (Love By Design Book 3)
- Protecting Bria (Special Force Operation Alphas)
- Protecting Chanel (Special Force Operation Alphas)
- Haven
- Taste (A New Adult romance)
- Sensual
- Seek To Please
- Seek To Bare
- Seek To Touch
- Seek To Love

- Seek To Trust
- Seek To Earn
- Protecting Yanira(Special Force Operation Alphas)

Thank you so much for reading and if you enjoyed the crazy ride and decide to leave a review we'd truly appreciate the support.

What's Next?!

Want to know what happens next?

Follow me on website to find out the latest about the next release.

Reviews are the lifeblood of the publishing world. They're read, appreciated, and needed. Please consider taking the time to leave a few words on Goodreads, or Bookbub.

Sign up for updates and sneak peeks at the site below.

304 Publishing Company

WE SHOWCASE AUTHORS writing African American, Interracial, Women's Fiction, Urban Romance, Erotic, and Contemporary Romance novels. Along with Thriller, Suspense, Poetry, Beauty, and Style Books. Thank you for taking the time out to visit. Join our mailing list to stay updated with new releases and blog posts.